PENGUIN BOOKS

SON OF SOUP

Rob Grant and Doug Naylor were part of the gestalt entity known as Grant Naylor, which created and wrote the Emmy award-winning series *Red Dwarf* for BBC television. Together they were head writers for *Spitting Image* in the mid-eighties, and together they wrote two novels, *Red Dwarf* and *Better Than Life*.

Since 1994 they have been pursuing separate careers. Doug wrote a third Red Dwarf novel, *Last Human*, which was a bestseller in 1995. All of these titles are published by Penguin. *Backwards*, Rob's bestselling new Red Dwarf book, was published by Viking in 1996.

ROB GRANT AND DOUG NAYLOR

Compiled and annotated by Rob Grant

SON OF SOUP

A SECOND SERVING OF THE LEAST WORST SCRIPTS

PENGUIN BOOKS

PENGUIN BOOKS

Published by the Penguin Group
Penguin Books Ltd, 27 Wrights Lane, London w8 5tz, England
Penguin Books USA Inc., 375 Hudson Street, New York, New York 10014, USA
Penguin Books Australia Ltd, Ringwood, Victoria, Australia
Penguin Books Canada Ltd, 10 Alcorn Avenue, Toronto, Ontario, Canada m4v 3b2
Penguin Books (NZ) Ltd, 182–190 Wairau Road, Auckland 10, New Zealand

Penguin Books Ltd, Registered Offices: Harmondsworth, Middlesex, England

First published in book form 1996
1 3 5 7 9 10 8 6 4 2

The moral right of the authors has been asserted

Set in 11/13pt Monotype Bembo
Typeset by Datix International Limited, Bungay, Suffolk
Printed in England by Clays Ltd, St Ives plc

CONTENTS

Introduction   vii

Boring Technical Bit   ix

Gunmen of the Apocalypse   1

Holoship   31

Camille   61

Backwards   85

Kryten   111

Me²   135

Credits   159

INTRODUCTION

This book contains a selection of scripts from *Red Dwarf*, one from each of its six seasons, presented, for reasons of perversity, in reverse order.

Gunmen of the Apocalypse, the world's first 'roast beef' western, was the show that represented the series for the Emmy award, and won. *Holoship*, from season five, was the longest recorded *Red Dwarf* episode ever – ten minutes had to be cut for transmission. The script is presented here in its original, over-long form, full of sequences and scenes now rotting in the Home for Unwanted Magnetic Tape. *Camille* and *Backwards* represent seasons three and four, and *Kryten* is the show that introduced the mechanoid with the over-active guilt chip.

And finally, from season one, *Me²*. This, the final show of the first season, was written almost a year after the rest of the shows – in fact, nearly four years after the pilot. Here's why.

The *Red Dwarf* pilot (*The End*) was submitted to the BBC in the summer of 1983. The BBC finally agreed to shoot the series in 1986. Five more scripts were completed and rehearsals began.

On the second day of rehearsals, the BBC electricians called a strike. No one was allowed through the picket lines to use the studios. In the expectation that the strike would be over by the end of the week, the *Red Dwarf* rehearsals continued. By the end of the week, the strike was still unsettled. Undaunted, we carried on rehearsing the second show, hoping to tack the first show on to the end of the recordings.

During week three, the strike carried on unabated. We rehearsed the third show, hoping to tack the first show on to the end of the recordings, and somehow squeeze the second show in somewhere along the way. By the fourth week, even the most optimistic of the production team was beginning to lose hope.

The strike was finally settled, but too late to save *Red Dwarf*. The production was abandoned, and nobody knew if the BBC would be prepared to pay the hideous cost of remounting it. There was serious doubt that *Red Dwarf* would ever make it to the screen.

For six months we waited. Finally, the BBC agreed to re-mount, and new recording dates were set for 1987.

The strike hadn't been all bad for the show. There had been a valuable opportunity to see the cast in action, and watch the bulk of the shows at least to rehearsal stage. The consensus was that the second show was the worst of the bunch. The story involved Rimmer trying to cope with his death by going insane, and trying to construct a new body for himself by stealing bits of Lister while he was asleep. We decided to replace it.

Me² was the replacement. It followed on from what had previously been the last show of the season, *Confidence and Paranoia*, which originally ended with Lister reviving his heart's desire, Kristine Kochanski, as a hologram. We rewrote the ending so that Lister was duped into duplicating Rimmer, to set up the final show, which was based on the notion that if you were forced to live with your exact replica, you might find out some fairly unpleasant things about yourself. Of course, the only way to have two Arnold Rimmers in one scene is to record it twice. Chris Barrie would play one half of the scene, then the tape would be rolled back, and he would play Rimmer 2 on the other side. This is a very difficult process for the actor – Chris almost killed himself in the scene where the two Rimmers are exercising. After take five, he was beginning to ask for a priest, and he isn't even Catholic – and very time-consuming for the technical bods. So, in order to render the script shootable in the available shooting time, a couple of the double Rimmer scenes had to be trimmed, and one dropped completely. Those scenes are reproduced here for the first time.

BORING TECHNICAL BIT

Wherever possible, we have tried to insert extra technical jargon into the scripts, to confuse and infuriate. See below.

INT.	**INT**erior.
EXT.	**EXT**erior.
OB	**O**utside **B**roadcast. (The scene is taped on location, not in the studio.)
PRE-VT	The scene is recorded before the main studio day, usually because it contains special effects that cannot be taped in front of a live audience.
POV	**P**oint **O**f **V**iew. E.g. 'Creature's POV' means the camera sees what the creature sees.
MIX TO	The outgoing shot dissolves into the incoming shot.
VO	**V**oice **O**ver. (The speaker is not in the shot.)
OOV	**O**ut **O**f **V**iew. (As above.)
SFX	Sound-effects.
Special FX	Special effects.
BEAT	Short pause.
DIST	**DIST**orted.
MIC	**MIC**rophone.
ATMOS	**ATMOS**phere. An indication that the sound engineers should play in a tape of appropriate background sounds.
SLO-MO	**SLO**w **MO**tion. A brilliant little abbreviation that saves the typist five keyboard presses.

SHOT	Camera **SHOT**. Tells the director where to point the camera when it's vital to the story or joke. Much hated by directors.
TWO-SHOT	Tells the director we need to see both the actors at this particular point. Even more hated by directors than SHOT.
CUT TO	Pointless direction to indicate the end of a scene.
MONTAGE	Indicates a sequence of scenes to be cut together, usually with music under, to establish passage of time and developing storylines. Directors quite like 'MONTAGE' because it credits them with some intelligence.
ADO	A digital effect whereby a camera shot is shrunk on the screen, then pasted onto another shot. In *Red Dwarf*, this is typically used to incorporate live action into model shots, or to put Holly's head into a shot where a genuine monitor isn't available.
O/S	Over-shoulder shot.
BLACK CYC	Black curtain, or a cheap way of having no set.
TAPE STOP	Stop recording while something is changed.
PULL OUT	Camera pulls back.

GUNMEN OF THE APOCALYPSE

1. Ext. Docks. Night

So dark and smoky we really can't make out much. Quayside sound-effects. A woman, LORETTA, walks through the fog, dressed in 1940s gear, carrying two suitcases. Suddenly, she is bathed in the glow of car headlights. The 1940s car stops and LISTER gets out, dressed in mac and hat, like a gumshoe.

LISTER: Maybe it's the moonlight, but I've got to admit, you're looking pretty good for a corpse.

LORETTA: Philip? I . . . I can explain everything.

LISTER: Let me save you the trouble. It was you who planned Pallister's murder, but it was your twin sister, Maxime who squibbed him off. You agreed to take the rap, knowing you'd the perfect alibi: me. That's why you came on so strong that night, playing me for the dumb sap I am.

LORETTA: Philip, it wasn't like that, not with you.

LISTER: Oh yeah?

LORETTA: (*suddenly scared*) So what are you going to do? Turn me in? Watch me do the sit-down dance in the electric chair at Sing Sing?

LISTER: No, sweetlips. I'm going to let you kiss me.

They lock in an embrace and kiss deeply.

2. Int. Ops room

LISTER *in the same stance, wearing an artificial reality outfit: head-piece, hand-piece, boots and groinal attachment, french-kissing thin air.*
KRYTEN *enters.*

KRYTEN: Sir, I think you should take a look at this.

LISTER *continues kissing, oblivious.*

KRYTEN: Sir? It really is quite urgent.

LISTER *breaks off the kiss and starts talking.*

LISTER: I want you, Loretta. I want your body next to mine. I want it like it was that Tuesday night. Kiss me.

LISTER *starts kissing again.*

KRYTEN: Honestly, sir, you haven't been off this machine in a month.

KRYTEN *grabs another helmet and starts putting it on.*

3. Ext. Docks. Night
LISTER *and* LORETTA *break off the embrace.*

LORETTA: Philip . . . I don't understand . . .
LISTER: It's simple, Loretta: this isn't real – it's an A/R computer simulation game, and I'm supposed to hand you over to the cops, and wind up with the goody-goody heroine. I've played it before, but you just drive me wild. You're the sexiest computer sprite I've ever seen.
LORETTA: Oh, Philip.
LISTER: I don't care that you've killed three men.
LORETTA: Five.
LISTER: Whatever. It's not your fault, it's just the way you're programmed.
LORETTA: And you're prepared to take me for what I am? A schizophrenic psychopathic serial-killing *femme fatale*?
LISTER: Forgive and forget, that's what I say. Pucker up.

They kiss again.

4. Int. Ops room

KRYTEN, *in helmet, boots and gloves, typing at a console marked 'Artificial Reality Console'. On the monitor, we read 'You are now entering Gumshoe – the A/R detective simulation. Choose your character.'*

KRYTEN: Choose your character? Honestly, I just want to speak to him. Anything . . . uhhhm . . . Sammy the Squib, hitman. Special skills . . . crackshot with tommy gun. Engage. (*Tuts*) So frivolous.

5. Ext. Docks. Night

KRYTEN *materializes, dressed like a forties gangster, carrying a violin case. He looks around. The place seems deserted.*

KRYTEN: Mr Lister? Sir?

KRYTEN *wheels round and spots the car, windows steamed up, rocking gently on its suspension.*

KRYTEN: Curious.

KRYTEN *peers in through the window, but can't see anything. He rubs away at the glass, to no avail. He raps at the window. The car stops rocking and the window is wound down. A very dishevelled* LISTER *pops his head out, wearing his hat and a string vest.*

LISTER: (*Embarrassed*) Oh, uh, hi, Kryters. What are you doing here?

KRYTEN: Sir, I've just got the results of the chemical scan. I discovered minute traces of millennium oxide in the local vicinity.

LISTER: I couldn't be more pleased for you. See you in an hour.

Starts to wind the window back up. KRYTEN *stops him.*

KRYTEN: Sir, I believe it means we've accidentally wandered into a rogue simulant hunting zone. That would explain the devastation on the derelict where we picked up this very game.

LORETTA: (*OOV*) Philip? Who is it?

LORETTA *pokes her head through the window.*

LORETTA: (*Terrified*) It's Sammy the Squib!

KRYTEN: Oh, uh, evening, Miss.

LORETTA: Don't kill me, Sammy, I'll do anything. Kill him (*Nods towards* LISTER). I'll come back to you. We'll run away together. It'll be like the old days. I never stopped loving you, Sammy. Kiss me.

LISTER: (*To* LORETTA) You're trash, aren't you?

LORETTA: I'm programmed to be trash.

LISTER: I can't resist her. Get back in the car.

LORETTA *goes OOV.*

LISTER: I never fall for women who are any good for me. It's either heartbreakers or moral garbage on legs.

KRYTEN: Sir, you have to turn off the A/R console. We have to shut down and continue on silent running, if we're to avoid detection.

LISTER *starts winding up the window.*

LISTER: Ten minutes.

KRYTEN: Sir . . .

LISTER: Five minutes. I'll keep my hat on.

Starts to wind up the window again.

KRYTEN: Now, sir.

LISTER *shakes his head and gets out of the car.*

LORETTA: Philip?

LISTER: I'll be back. Stay bad.

LISTER *and* KRYTEN *clap their hands and vanish.*

6. Int. Ops room

LISTER *and* KRYTEN *slip off their A/R helmets.*

LISTER: Kryten, you're a total gooseberry. Next time I go on the A/R machine, I'm going to give you some money and send you off to the pictures.

7. Int. Cockpit

CAT *piloting,* RIMMER *at his station. The lights dim and console lights flick out as* Starbug *powers down.*

RIMMER: At last! We have silent running. OK, long-range scanners are down. The only early warning we've got is you. Stay alert.

CAT: OK, bud. I'll keep my nose peeled.

RIMMER *steps down to:*

8. Int. Mid-section

And starts to check the monitor there as KRYTEN *and* LISTER *come down from the ops room.* KRYTEN *crosses to cockpit.*

RIMMER: You took your time. (*To* LISTER) Where've you been?

LISTER: I was in the A/R machine.

RIMMER: Again?

LISTER: What d'you mean 'again'?

RIMMER: Everybody knows you only use the A/R machine to have sex.

LISTER: Not true.

RIMMER: Yes, true. It's pathetic watching you grind away on your own, day after day. You look like a dog that's missing its master's leg. That groinal attachment's supposed to have a lifetime guarantee. You've nearly worn it out in three weeks.

LISTER: That is a scandalous, outrageous piece of libel. I don't just play the Role Play games. What about the sporting simulations? Zero Gee, Kick Boxing, Wimbledon . . .

RIMMER: You only play Wimbledon because you're having it off with that jailbait ball girl.

LISTER: Another total lie. She is not jailbait. She's seventeen.

RIMMER: She's a computer sprite, Lister, and surely that's the point. She's just a load of pixels.

LISTER: But what pixels!

And they step up to:

9. Int. Cockpit

RIMMER *and* LISTER *take up their stations.*

LISTER: So what's all the hullabaloo?

CAT: We've wandered into rogue simulant country.

KRYTEN: Bio-mechanical warriors, created for a war that never took place. A number of them escaped the dismantling program, and now prowl Deep Space, in search of quarry worthy of their mettle.

RIMMER: I say we abandon pursuit of *Red Dwarf*, and flee from the zone.

LISTER: Give up the chase? You're kidding?

CAT: My nose is getting something.

KRYTEN: Powering up.

Lights change, powering up SFX. They all turn to their monitors.

RIMMER: Scanners report a battle-class cruiser on intercept.

KRYTEN: It's rogue simulants all right.

RIMMER: They've got enough hardware on board that thing to blast our smithereens to smithereens. Recommend immediate, total and unequivocal surrender.

KRYTEN: Sir – surrender is the worst thing we could do. They despise humans and all forms of humanoid life. (*To* LISTER) They believe you to be the vermin of the universe.

CAT: Didn't even know they'd met him.

KRYTEN: Getting a message. Punching it up.

On the monitor:

10. Int. Black cyc.

TWO ROGUE SIMULANTS *talk straight to camera, with a light pallet behind them.*

SIMULANT CAPTAIN: State your species and purpose.

11. Int. Cockpit

RIMMER: One of us will have to speak to them. Who's the least human-looking? (*Pause*) Listy, the mic's all yours.

LISTER: Wait a minute, stall them with static, I've got an idea. Kryten, mid-section. Cat, you too.

LISTER, CAT *and* KRYTEN *exit to mid-section.*

12. Model shot

The battle-cruiser looms over Starbug.

13. Int. Cockpit

In the monitor, the TWO SIMULANTS *reappear.*

SIMULANT CAPTAIN: Why do you delay? State your species and purpose. You have one minute.

RIMMER: (*Calls*) Lister, what the hell are you doing?

LISTER: (*Off*) OK. Almost ready. Stand by to transmit.

14. Int. Black cyc

O/S *of the* TWO ROGUE SIMULANTS *as they look into a monitor.*

FEMALE SIMULANT: Incoming.

The monitor comes to life. What appears to be a strange alien life-form comes on to screen. It is, in fact, the bottom half of LISTER*'s face, shot upside down below the nose. Taped to his chin are two antennae made out of pipe-cleaners with Kryten's spare eyes glued to the end.*

LISTER: Greetings. I am Tarka Dhal, an ambassador of the Great Vindalooian Empire.

SIMULANT CAPTAIN: Our scanners reported human life on your vessel? Is this so?

LISTER: Humans!? (*Mimes spit.*) The Vindalooian people despise all humans. They are the vermin of the universe. (*Turns.*) Are they not, Bhindi Bajhii?

The upside-down CAT's *face slides on to the screen.*

CAT: You bet. We just hate them. Scum, scum, scum, scum, scum.

LISTER: The Vindalooian Empire is pledged to exterminate them all . . .

15. Int. Mid-section

LISTER *and* CAT *lying on a bench looking up at a wall-mounted video camera.*

LISTER: . . . and we will not rest until this task is completed.

The SIMULANT CAPTAIN *materializes in the mid-section.* CAT *and* LISTER *oblivious.*

LISTER: To the glory of all Vindalooia! We bid you farewell and safe passage.

RIMMER: Uh, Lister . . .

CAT: And if you come across any of that humanoid garbage, send them our loathing, and torture one for me!

LISTER *and* CAT *laugh. They suddenly become aware that the* SIMU-LANT CAPTAIN *is looming over them, carrying a gun.* LISTER *and the* CAT *stand with the pipe-cleaners stuck on the end of their chins, and try to smile winningly.*

LISTER: Hi.

CAT: How's it going, bud?

SIMULANT CAPTAIN: A human and a humanoid. A hologra-matic human. And a mechanoid who is a slave to humans. I had hoped for so much more.

SIMULANT CAPTAIN *starts examining the facilities.*

RIMMER: I have no idea who you are, but boarding this vessel is an act of war. Ergo, we surrender, and as prisoners of war, I invoke Article five seven four three two eight seven six five stroke B of the All Nations Agreement.

KRYTEN: Article five seven four three two eight seven six five stroke B? 'Each Nation attending the conference is only allocated one car-parking space'? Is that absolutely relevant? I mean, we're in mortal danger, and you're worried about the Chinese delegates bringing two cars!

RIMMER: Can't you let just *one* go? I was talking about the right of POWs to non-violent constraint.

KRYTEN: But that's seven six five stroke *C*!

RIMMER: It's embarrassing as much as anything else. You're totally humiliating me in front of this xenophobic genocidal maniac. (*To* SIMULANT) No offence.

SIMULANT CAPTAIN *turns from the computer banks.*

SIMULANT CAPTAIN: Primitive. You will be no sport at all. I have no alternative.

SIMULANT CAPTAIN *raises his gun and fires a bolt at each of them.* CAT, LISTER *and* KRYTEN *fall.* RIMMER*'s light bee hits the deck.*

16. Model shot
Starbug *and battle-cruiser side by side in space.*

17. Int. Cockpit
Close-up on LISTER *as he comes to, at his station, head on the console.* CAT *and* KRYTEN*, in their seats, are beginning to stir. Suddenly the light bee on Rimmer's seat levitates and* RIMMER *materializes around it.*

RIMMER: How long have we been out?

LISTER: According to the NaviComp, three weeks.

KRYTEN: Strange. The drive interface has been upgraded. So have the engines.

RIMMER: And if this read-out's correct, we're armed. Laser cannons.

LISTER: They've totally upgraded the whole ship.

CAT: What technology. They even got rid of the squeak on the seat tilt control.

SIMULANT CAPTAIN *appears on the monitor.* FEMALE SIMULANT *beside him.*

SIMULANT CAPTAIN: We have made some improvements to your craft. Now, at least, you may prove to be of some small amusement.

FEMALE SIMULANT: You have two Earth minutes before we attack.

Monitor blinks off.

RIMMER: Let's get out of here.

CAT: Wait. I know this game: it's called Cat and Mouse. There's only one way to win it: don't be the mouse.

LISTER: What are you saying?

CAT: I'm saying: the mouse never wins. Not unless you believe those lying cartoons! We don't run, we strike. It's the last thing they'll be expecting.

RIMMER: No, the last thing they'll be expecting is for us to turn into ice-skating mongooses and dance the Bolero. And your plan makes about as much sense.

LISTER: Well, I say go with it.

KRYTEN: Agreed.

CAT: You're gonna go with one of my plans? Are you nuts? What happens if we all get killed – I'll never hear the last of it.

CAT *starts up the engines.*

18. Model shot
Starbug *powers off away from the battle-cruiser, then suddenly arcs back towards it.*

19. Int. Black cyc
O/S: the TWO SIMULANTS *turn to the monitor.* Starbug *heading towards them.*

SIMULANT CAPTAIN: What are they doing? Power up the weapons, raise the –

There is an explosion just in front of camera.

20. Model shot
Starbug *strafes the battle-cruiser, causing terminal damage.*

21. Int. Cockpit
ALL *at their stations.*

LISTER: Nailed them!

22. Int. Black cyc
Fire, smoke and explosions. On the monitor, Starbug *is getting away.*

SIMULANT CAPTAIN: Damage report.
FEMALE SIMULANT: Fluke hit. They penetrated the engine core. Fifteen seconds to meltdown.
SIMULANT CAPTAIN: Take them with us.
FEMALE SIMULANT: Central weapons bank is down. We can't return fire.
SIMULANT CAPTAIN: Then they'll find our corpse has a sting in its tail. Hack into their navigation computer. Transmit the Armageddon virus.

23. Int. Cockpit
They are all watching their monitors at the stricken ship. Suddenly, the console in front of KRYTEN *sparks and fizzles.*

LISTER: What is it?
KRYTEN: The NaviComp. Something's wrong.

The SIMULANT CAPTAIN *appears on the monitor.*

SIMULANT CAPTAIN: See you in Silicon Hell.

Explosion fills the screen.

24. Model shot

Cruiser explodes, leaving devastated hulk.

25. Int. Cockpit

The NaviComp is fizzing and sparking.

CAT: The controls are locked.

KRYTEN: Shutdown all network links. The NaviComp's been infected with a virus.

KRYTEN *and* LISTER *flick switches desperately.*

CAT: Which means what?

LISTER: The NaviComp's frozen us out. We're locked on this course. (*To* RIMMER) If we carry on straight ahead at this speed, how long before we hit trouble?

RIMMER: Well if you define trouble as a rather large moon directly in our path, approximately thirty-eight minutes.

KRYTEN: The only solution is for me to contract the virus myself, analyse its structure and attempt to create a software antidote before it wipes out my core program. Do I have your permission to sacrifice myself, sirs?

RIMMER: Do lemmings like cliffs? Granted.

KRYTEN *plugs himself into the NaviComp.*

KRYTEN: I'm going to have to design a dove program.

CAT: Dove program?

KRYTEN: A dove program spreads peace through the system, obliterating the viral cells as it goes.

Suddenly KRYTEN *judders and fizzes as he contracts the virus.*

KRYTEN: I have it.

KRYTEN *jerks and sparks.*

KRYTEN: The virus is extremely complex. I must devote all my run time to the solution. Shutting down all non-essential systems.

LISTER: Can we help? Is there something we can do?

KRYTEN: Watch my dreams.

KRYTEN *shuts down his systems and we cut to:*

26. Int. Ops room

KRYTEN *lies on the light-slab. Various wires lead from him to monitors.* LISTER *is plugging leads into* KRYTEN*'s chest.* CAT *is scanning the monitors.* RIMMER *enters.*

RIMMER: Twenty-three minutes to impact. Any change?

LISTER: He's getting worse. Weaker and weaker.

RIMMER: Look, sooner or later we're going to have to face the fact that we're not all getting out of this in one piece. Or, if we are, it's going to be one big flat piece.

LISTER: And?

RIMMER: I think it's time for us to decide who's going to take the one-man escape pod.

CAT: How?

RIMMER: Well, if you'll just bear with me, I believe I've devised a fair and equitable system for choosing who should survive. It's based on experience, rank, seniority, blah, blah, blah. To cut a long story short . . . it's me. I was as stunned as you are, which is why I demanded a recount. But, blow me if it didn't come out as me again. So where are the keys?

LISTER: Rimmer – the escape pod's not an option.

RIMMER: Why would that be?

LISTER: It escaped last Thursday. I was having a few beers, couldn't be bothered moving. So I used the release mechanism as a bottle opener.

RIMMER: That's it then. We're finished.

CAT: Wait a minute. Getting something.

Suddenly the screen crackles and we hear distant honky-tonk piano music and saloon bar atmos. LISTER *joins* CAT *and* RIMMER *and they watch the monitor. The picture clears and we see:*

27. OB. Ext. Street of Laredo. Day

Wide-shot of the street. We hear the saloon merriment. A stagecoach rolls past camera.

CAT: (*VO*) What is this?

LISTER: (*VO*) I think we've tapped directly into whatever passes for Kryten's subconscious.

We see a sign: 'Sheriff's Office'. The sheriff's door opens and out steps KRYTEN. *He is wearing a filthy, bedraggled old cowboy outfit, hat and sheriff's star. He stands strangely erect, clearly drunk, trying to act sober. He finishes off the last half-sip in an empty liquor bottle, throws it aside, so it smashes, and tries to cross the street as best he can.*

CAT: (*VO*) Why is he a sheriff in some old western?

LISTER: (*VO*) Must be how his core program is coping with the battle against the virus. For whatever reason, it's converted his struggle into some kind of dream.

KRYTEN *staggers towards the saloon. He passes a wanted poster on the saloon front: 'Wanted – Dead or Alive. The Four Apocalypse Boys'.* KRYTEN *throws open the saloon doors and strides in.*

28. Int. Saloon. Day

Busy. COWBOYS *playing poker,* SALOON GIRLS, *etc. A* PIANO PLAYER *plays honky tonk version of* Red Dwarf *theme.* KRYTEN *tries to steer his way towards the bar. He passes* JIMMY, *a smooth oaf, playing cards with some unruly* COWPOKES.

JIMMY: Well, well, well, Sheriff – fancy seein' a man of your sober disposition in a low-down drinking establishment.

EVERYONE *laughs.*

KRYTEN: Now, boys, I don't want any trouble. I'm just doing my rounds.

JIMMY *sticks out a foot and trips him over.* EVERYONE *laughs.* KRYTEN *drags himself up.*

KRYTEN: You shouldn't ought to have done that, Jimmy.

Piano music stops. People get out of the way, ready for a gunfight. JIMMY *stands, ready to draw.*

JIMMY: Why don't you try it, Sheriff? They say you used to be faster than a toilet stop in rattlesnake country.

KRYTEN *thinks about going for his gun, but* . . .

KRYTEN: Sorry I stumbled over your boot, Jimmy, sir. I didn't mean anything by it.

EVERYONE *laughs. Piano music starts up again.* KRYTEN *walks to the bar.*

KRYTEN: Give me two fingers of your best sipping liquor, Miss Lola. And I want the smooth stuff. The stuff where you get your eyesight back after two days, guaranteed.

LOLA *the bartender sets down a tot glass and pours some whisky into it. As* KRYTEN *reaches for the drink,* JIMMY *calls back from the saloon doors.*

JIMMY: The Apocalypse Boys is here!

Suddenly the piano stops and EVERYONE *dives under tables and cowers out of sight.* KRYTEN *is standing alone at the bar.*

JIMMY: They's askin' for you, Sheriff.

KRYTEN *hoists up his drink and downs it.*

KRYTEN: (*Scared*) I'll be right out.

KRYTEN *walks towards the doors, pausing to drink a few other people's whisky on his way. He picks up a fullish bottle from a table near the doors and staggers out into the street.*

29. OB. Ext. Street of Laredo. Day
Outside the saloon, the cowboy version of the FOUR HORSEMEN OF THE APOCALYPSE *wait on their mounts, leaning casually on their saddles.*

KRYTEN: I don't believe I've had the pleasure, sirs.

DEATH *spits out some chewing tobacco, which fizzles on the street like acid.*

DEATH: The name's Death. And these here're my brothers. Brother War . . .

WAR *laughs and flames shoot out of his mouth.*

DEATH: . . . Brother Famine . . .

Fat FAMINE *nods and takes a bite of chicken.*

DEATH: . . . and Brother Pestilence.

PESTILENCE *grins: horrible broken teeth. He swipes idly at the swarm of buzzing flies around his head.*

KRYTEN: Well, you seem like a nice neighbourly bunch of boys. How can I be of service?

ALL FOUR *apocalypse boys draw, shoot* KRYTEN*'s hat off, his bottle out of his hand, and he dances around trying to avoid the hail of bullets. Finally the gunfire stops.*

DEATH: We want your sorry ass out of here. You got one hour.

DEATH *spits a sizzler again, and* THE FOUR HORSEMEN *turn and trot off, passing under a dangling sign: 'You are now leaving Existence'. And as the* HORSEMEN *ride under it, they disappear.* KRYTEN *takes off his sheriff's star and throws it on the floor.*

30. Int. Ops room
KRYTEN *on the light-slab.*

LISTER: He's losing the battle. Look at his lifesigns. They're barely registering.
CAT: Is there any way we could get in there and help him? Some-how turn ourselves into tiny electronic people and get into his

dream? Haven't we got some kind of gizmo lying around someplace that could do that? And if not, (*bangs the table angrily*) why not?

RIMMER: (*To* CAT) Look, we've all got something to bring to this discussion, and I think from now on, the thing you should bring is silence.

LISTER: No, maybe he's got something.

CAT: Twice in one lifetime? When you're hot, you're hot!

LISTER: Look, if we link up the Artificial Reality console to Kryten's mind, then we should be able to project straight into his dreamstate like it's a normal computer game.

CAT: What did I tell you? We don't even have to leave the room.

LISTER *opens a locker and digs out some Artificial-Reality outfits.*

RIMMER: What about me?

LISTER: We'll shut down all extraneous systems and power up your hard light drive. (*Tosses* CAT *a helmet*) Come on – let's get them wagons rolling.

31. Int. Ops room

LISTER, CAT *and* RIMMER *in A/R helmets, gloves, boots and groinal attachments, visors raised.* LISTER *is tapping the A/R console.*

LISTER: OK, I've loaded the characters from a western A/R game. Choose a player, One to Three.

CAT: Two.

LISTER: You're the Riviera Kid. Special skills: ace gunslinger. Rimmer?

RIMMER: Uno.

LISTER: You are Dangerous Dan McGrew. Special skills: barefist fighting. Which leaves me with Brett Riverboat: knifeman. Ye-es.

RIMMER: And we definitely can't get hurt?

LISTER: It's just like a computer game. You can leave any time you want. There's a button on the palm of your glove. Just clap your hands, and you're out.

LISTER *claps his gloved hands like a Spanish fandango dancer.*

LISTER: OK, Riviera, Dangerous – let's mosey on into town.

They ALL *flip down their visors and:*

32. OB. Ext. Street of Laredo. Day
Through a swirling mist, LISTER, CAT *and* RIMMER *ride into town, dressed as cool dude cowboys.* PASSERS-BY *give them scared looks.* LISTER *nods towards the saloon.*

33. Int. Saloon
As before. Much merriment. LISTER, CAT *and* RIMMER *enter. Piano stops. Everyone stops talking.*

RIMMER: I've seen westerns, I know how to speak cowboy. Leave the talking to me.

They stride up to the bar.

RIMMER: Dry white wine and Perrier, please.

LISTER *and* CAT *close their eyes in quiet exasperation.*

RIMMER: And what about you two chaps?
LISTER: Rimmer – what westerns have you seen? Butch Accountant and the Yuppie Kid?
CAT: Leave it to me. This is one for the Riviera Kid.

CAT *does Riviera Kid dance.*

CAT: (*To* LOLA) Three shots of gulping whisky, Ma'am.

LOLA *pours three shots.* LISTER *and* CAT *toss it straight back.*

LISTER: (*Putting on a brave face*) Mighty smooth.
CAT: (*Ditto*) I was expecting something with a little more kick to it.

LISTER *and* CAT *look at* RIMMER, *who looks at the whisky.*

RIMMER: I don't suppose you've got any ginger ale mixers? No? No matter. I'll take it neat, then.

RIMMER *downs the shot. He smiles, looks a little queasy. We realize he's going to be sick. He grabs the hat from a nearby* COWPOKE *and is ill into it. Music and talk stop. The* COWPOKE *stands. He's a very big cowpoke. Chairs scrape back from tables.*

COWPOKE: A man beans up in the hat of Bearstrangler McGee is either mighty brave, or mighty stupid. Which are you, boy?

RIMMER: Sorry, what were the choices again?

LISTER: You'll have to forgive our friend. He's ... *(indicates 'simple')* a couple of gunmen short of a posse.

LISTER *hands* COWPOKE *some banknotes.*

COWPOKE: That pays for the hat. What about the insult?

RIMMER: An insult? OK, you're a fat, bearded git with breath that could concuss a grizzly.

LISTER *hastily hands over more banknotes.*

LISTER: Take the lot, man.

LISTER *takes* RIMMER *aside.*

LISTER: Rimmer, what is wrong with you?

RIMMER: Relax. You said yourself no one can hurt us. Besides, you're forgetting I'm Dangerous Dan McGrew, barefist fighter extraordinaire.

LISTER *nods towards the doors.* KRYTEN *enters the saloon, wearing a dirty old long trail coat, carrying a small box containing his possessions, and goes up to the bar.*

KRYTEN: Miss Lola, all my valuables are here in this box. You can have it all for just one bottle of mind-rotter.

LOLA *looks in the box and takes out a magnificent pair of ivory-handled six-guns.*

LOLA: You're trading in your shooting-irons?

KRYTEN: No use to me. I've got the shakes worse than two porcupines on their wedding night.

LOLA *pulls out an apple and a bunch of carrots.*

LOLA: Carrots?
KRYTEN: I'm throwing in my mule, Dignity.
RIMMER: (*Sotto*) Mr Sad Git or what?
LISTER: Kryten? It's us, man.
KRYTEN: Sorry, friend. Don't believe I've had the pleasure.

LOLA *puts a bottle on the bar.* KRYTEN *looks at it with obscene lust.*

LISTER: Kryten – don't you know who we are? Why you're here?

KRYTEN *swigs from the bottle.*

LISTER: You're fighting an electronic virus. You're trying to create a dove program, some kind of software antidote to wipe it out.
KRYTEN: I'll drink to that.

KRYTEN *swigs again.*

CAT: Listen to him, hooch head! The virus is winning. You've got to get your head together and start fighting it.

Suddenly we hear a whiplash, and the bottle is yanked out of KRYTEN'*s grasp.* KRYTEN *turns to see* JIMMY *dangling the bottle at the end of a long whip.*

JIMMY: Want a drink, Sheriff? Why don't you come and take one?
KRYTEN: Now, Jimmy, there's no call to be making me look foolish.

KRYTEN *makes a grab at the bottle, but* JIMMY *yanks it out of reach.*

JIMMY: Come on, Sheriff, jump. You can git higher than that.

Jimmy's CRONIES *laugh.*

LISTER: Leave him alone.

Music stops. Everyone stops talking and scrapes back their chairs, ready for a fight.

JIMMY: Just havin' us a little fun, Mr Swanky Pants.

LISTER *takes a knife from inside his jacket.*

LISTER: Brett Riverboat, knifeman. Let's see how good you are.

LISTER *throws the knife, severing the whip and freeing the bottle.* KRYTEN *catches it.* LISTER *grins.* JIMMY *goes for his gun, but a second knife pins his right sleeve to the wall.*

JIMMY: Son of a –

JIMMY *reaches for his other gun, but a third knife pins his left sleeve to the wall.* LISTER *picks up the apple from* KRYTEN*'s box and throws it. It lodges in* JIMMY*'s mouth.* LISTER *turns back to the bar. The piano starts up and everyone starts talking again.* JIMMY *spits out the apple.*

JIMMY: Frank . . . Nuke.

Two mean-looking GUNMEN *step forward.*

JIMMY: Line his lungs with lead.

CAT *steps out.*

JIMMY: Who in the heck are you?
CAT: They call me the Kid. The Riviera Kid.

CAT *does Riviera Kid dance.*

JIMMY: Well, Riviera Kid. I hope your shootin's as fancy as your dancin'.

SLO-MO: FRANK *and* NUKE *go for their guns and shoot once each. Back to the* CAT*, who casually draws and fires twice. There are two mid-air flashes halfway between* CAT *and the gunfighters, and two bullets clatter to the floor.* JIMMY *picks one up.*

JIMMY: He shot your damn bullets out of the air.

CAT *spins his guns and holsters them.*

KRYTEN: Well, it's been dandy meeting you boys, but if I'm not out of here by sundown, the buzzards will be fighting the lizards for my gizzards.

KRYTEN *exits.*

LISTER: If he leaves town, we're dead. Stop him.

LISTER, CAT *and* RIMMER *make for the door.* JIMMY *and his* CRO-NIES *part to let them through, but as* RIMMER *passes,* ONE OF THE CRONIES *goes to smash him over the head with a chair.* RIMMER *goes into action: lays out the first* CRONY, *karate-kicks a* SECOND, *despatches a* THIRD *with a pool cue, and throws a* FOURTH *over the bar.*

RIMMER: Marvellous.

34. OB. Ext. Street of Laredo. Day

KRYTEN *is halfway down the street as* LISTER, CAT *and* RIMMER *dash out of the bar.*

CAT: Hey, buddy!
RIMMER: Hold it!

KRYTEN *looks back, then speeds up.*

LISTER: You've got to stay!

KRYTEN *starts to run towards the 'You are now leaving Existence' sign.* LISTER, CAT *and* RIMMER *start to chase him.*

CAT: Leave this to the Riviera Kid.

CAT *does Riviera Kid dance, draws his gun, aims his gun to the side and fires behind his back. The bullet hits a tin bath and ricochets across the street, where it hits a bell and ricochets again. Wide-shot of street as the bullet zig-zags towards* KRYTEN, *finally severing the support on one side of the dangling 'Existence' sign, which swings down and flattens* KRYTEN. LISTER, CAT *and* RIMMER *run up to him.*

KRYTEN: You don't understand, boys. I've got to leave. Look . . . (*takes out pocket watch – we don't see its face*) ten to death.

LISTER: OK, we've got ten minutes to sober him up and get him in shape.

35. Int. Saloon

SHOT: spoon dipping into a bowl of raw ground coffee. Follow the spoon to KRYTEN *'s mouth. The saloon is now deserted.*

KRYTEN: I just can't eat any more raw coffee.

LISTER: Two more bowls.

LISTER *tops up the bowl from a jar.* KRYTEN *pushes bowl away.*

KRYTEN: Honest, I'm sober.

LISTER: OK, who are you? What are you doing here?

KRYTEN: It's like you say. I'm some kind of robot, who's fighting this virus, and none of this exists, it's some kind of fever, except for you guys, who do exist, only you're not really here, you're really on some spaceship in the future. (*BEAT*) Hell, if that's got to make sense, I don't want to *be* sober.

The CAT *comes up, carrying Kryten's guns.*

CAT: Got his guns back. Look at the handles. They've got little doves carved on 'em. And check this.

CAT *snaps open gun.*

CAT: There's no place for the bullets to go.

LISTER *takes the guns.*

LISTER: This is it, Kryten. The answer's in these guns, somehow. Doves. Dove program.

LISTER *hands the guns to* KRYTEN *, who turns them over in his hands.*

KRYTEN: I just don't know. I . . . I . . .

We hear the courthouse bell clang.

KRYTEN: Wait a minute – I think I'm beginning to remember some things. (*To* LISTER) You. Every time I look at you, I get an image of curries and morning breath that could cut through bank vaults. (*To* RIMMER) And you, sir, you seem familiar, too. I keep getting a name. Smee . . . Smee-hee . . .?

RIMMER: Smeghead?

KRYTEN: That's it!

RIMMER: (*Excited*) He remembers me!

LISTER: And the guns? Do they mean anything to you?

KRYTEN: Something. They mean something. If I had more time . . .

The CAT *looks back from the saloon doors.*

CAT: Company.

KRYTEN *leads them out into the street.*

36. OB. Ext. Street of Laredo. Day

The APOCALYPSE BOYS *walk slowly through the swirling mist and stop.* KRYTEN *steps out to face them.* LISTER, RIMMER *and* CAT *file out after him and they fan out across the street.*

DEATH: Got yourself a little help, Sheriff?

KRYTEN: Now I remember. You're a computer virus. You travel from machine to machine, overwriting the core program.

DEATH: Have infection will travel, that's me. Let's see if we can't tip the balance a little, here.

DEATH *holds up his arms. A bolt of blue electricity shoots up into the sky. MIX to:*

37. Int. Ops room

A blue spark shoots out of KRYTEN'*s head and travels up the wire connecting him to the A/R console. The console fizzles like the Navi-Comp did before, and we see the monitor screen: 'Special skills' and, flashing beside it, 'Erase'.*

38. OB. Ext. Street of Laredo. Day
As before.

CAT: What's he doing?

RIMMER: He's stalling. He spotted us for what we are: a bunch of mean, macho, bad-ass desperadoes who are about to kick his bony butt clean across the Pecos. (*Throws toothpick to the ground.*) Enjoy the show.

RIMMER *strides off.*

LISTER: (*To* CAT) Cover him.

CAT: Sounds like a job for the Riviera Kid.

CAT *does Riviera Kid dance, then tries to draw his guns, but fumbles them both. He grabs at them, but they fall into a puddle.*

CAT: Hot damn! I've lost my special skill!

RIMMER: Who's got the guts to go with me one on one? Hand to hand? *Mano a mano?*

WAR *steps forward and bellows fire threateningly. He turns and rips a support post from the boardwalk.* RIMMER *tries to rip one from the other side, can't budge it. Unperturbed, he spits on his hands and tries again. As* WAR *advances on* RIMMER, LISTER *takes out a knife and tries to throw it, but it flies off sideways, jamming into a post.*

LISTER: (*Calls*) Rimmer! The virus has spread to the Artificial Reality unit. It's taken away our special skills.

RIMMER *turns and faces* WAR.

RIMMER: Ah. Mr War, sir. It would appear that, due to circumstances completely beyond my control, there's been a bit of a cock-up in the bravado department.

WAR *smashes* RIMMER *with the post.* RIMMER *goes down and gets up again.*

RIMMER: I may indeed have come over as being a little bit more brave than in fact I am.

LISTER: (*Calls*) Exit! Exit!

RIMMER *claps his hands. Nothing happens. He claps again. Nothing.* WAR *whacks him again.* RIMMER *gets up and leaps about, clapping his hands like a Spanish fandango dancer.* LISTER *and* CAT *also leap about, trying to clap their hands, as* WAR *swings at them with the post.*

LISTER: We're sealed in.
CAT: Get the helmets off!

LISTER, RIMMER *and* CAT *struggle to pull off their (invisible to us) helmets, their faces stretching and straining.*

RIMMER: It won't move.
LISTER: There's a clasp at the back!

39. Int. Ops room

LISTER, CAT *and* RIMMER *struggling with the A/R helmets. The* CAT *manages to tear off one of his A/R gloves.*

40. OB. Ext. Street of Laredo. Day

LISTER, RIMMER *and* CAT *still straining.*

CAT: I got one of the gloves off.

We see CAT*'s arm dangling loosely by his side, as he hops around on one foot, trying to pull the A/R boot off.*

CAT: And a boot, too!

The CAT *loses all control of his left side.*

RIMMER: Oh, brilliant! Now you're completely paralysed down your left side.
LISTER: You've got to get your helmet off first. Help me find the clasp.

WAR *whacks* RIMMER*. The* CAT *starts pulling* LISTER*'s head from under the chin.*

LISTER: I can't breathe.
CAT: I think I got it!

LISTER: You're strangling me.

CAT: Here it comes.

LISTER: Cat, I can't –

CAT *falls backwards,* LISTER *disappears.*

41. Int. Ops room

LISTER *gets up from the floor, minus his A/R helmet, and starts unplugging the others.*

42. OB. Ext. Street of Laredo. Day

All FOUR APOCALYPSE BOYS *form a semi-circle around the half-paralysed* CAT *and, behind him, the cowering* RIMMER. *They advance slowly, holding huge Bowie knives.*

DEATH: We're gonna slice you up so small, the worms won't even have to chew.

The CAT *disappears.*

RIMMER: You can't frighten me – I'm a coward, I'm always scared. Lister!!

As the GUNMEN *lunge their blades at him,* RIMMER *vanishes.*

43. Int. Ops room

RIMMER, *hands in the air, his face contorted, shielding himself from the blow.*

CAT: Now what?

LISTER: It's down to Kryten.

And RIMMER *joins them at the monitor, on which we see:*

44. OB. Ext. Street of Laredo. Day

The FOUR GUNMEN, *grouped where we left them. They turn and face* KRYTEN *who is standing halfway down the street.*

DEATH: Well, Sheriff. Now it's just li'l ol' you.

KRYTEN: I'm not afraid, Mr Death, sir, I believe my colleagues bought me enough time to complete the antidote program. Now, if you'll forgive the rather confrontational imperative: go for your guns, you scum-sucking molluscs!

SLO-MO: The GUNMEN *all draw and fire.* KRYTEN *gets hit four times. He staggers, then straightens, and draws both guns. As the guns leave his holster and he raises them, they both transform into* WHITE DOVES, *which fly off into the sky. The* GUNMEN *collapse and die, then slowly fade away.*

45. Int. Ops room

KRYTEN, *still on the bench, opens his eyes.*

KRYTEN: I did it! I created the antidote.

LISTER: Impact in two minutes.

46. Model shot

Starbug *diving into an atmosphere.*

47. Int. Cockpit

LISTER, CAT *and* RIMMER *stumble in after* KRYTEN, *who starts plugging himself into the NaviComp.*

RIMMER: How long will it take?

KRYTEN: Just a matter of seconds. How long to impact?

RIMMER: Just a matter of seconds.

KRYTEN: There it goes. I've released it into the NaviComp.

Computer starts clicking on.

RIMMER: Eight seconds. Seven . . .

KRYTEN: We're almost there.

CAT: Five . . .

48. Model shot

Starbug *diving towards a bubbling, glowing lava sea.*

49. Int. Cockpit

CAT: Three . . . two . . .

LISTER: We're not going to make it.

CAT: Impact!

50. Model shot

Starbug *crashes into boiling lava sea. There is a pause. A long pause. Then* Starbug *bursts out to triumphant* Red Dwarf *western music.*

ALL: (*VO*) Yeeeh-hawww!!!

51. Model shot

Red Dwarf *flies off into the sunset as the* Big Country-*type* Red Dwarf *theme plays over:*

Credits

HOLOSHIP

1. Model shot
Starbug *in space. MIX TO:*

2. Int. *Starbug* rear. Night

The lights are down. KRYTEN, LISTER, *the* CAT *and* RIMMER *are watching a movie on an unseen TV. We pan along their reactions as the music swells, and we hear dialogue from the screen.*

ACTOR: (*Tearful*) Oh Marnie . . .

ACTRESS: Oh my darling – don't! This isn't a time for sadness – it's a time for joy, for laughter. Don't you see: whatever this crazy old world throws at us now, it doesn't matter, none of it.

ACTOR: But, Marnie, we can never be together again!

ACTRESS: Oh, my darling, you're wrong. You're so wrong. So, so wrong. We'll always be together – It's just . . . we'll be apart.

The music swells to a climax. The lights remain dimmed.

KRYTEN: Oh, that was just beautiful. Well recommended, sir.

LISTER: (*Trying to hide the fact that he's been crying*) Mnhhh.

KRYTEN: D'you think they ever met again?

LISTER: (*Tries, in blubber-speak, to say 'Don't know', but it comes out*) Mnuh mnoh.

KRYTEN: Pardon?

LISTER: (*Blubber-speak*) Mnuh mnohhhhhh.

KRYTEN: (*To* RIMMER) Didn't you think it was just wonderful, sir? The way he sacrificed his career, his dreams, everything for the woman he loved.

RIMMER: I thought it was the worst pile of blubbery schoolgirl mush I've ever been compelled to endure. I consider it an insult to my backside that it was forced to sit here growing carbuncles through that putrid adolescent slush.

KRYTEN: You didn't find it uplifting?

RIMMER: It was not in the least bit uplifting. It was totally unbelievable. Why would he give up everything for a woman he's never going to see again?

KRYTEN: Because she loved him, and he would have that for ever. (*To* LISTER) Isn't that right, sir?

LISTER: (*Blows his nose and nods his head.*)

CAT: Personally, I thought it started well, but fell apart. All the stuff with the ducks all getting into trouble, that was great. Then it all went black and white, and I just fell asleep.

KRYTEN: Sir, that was the cartoon before the main programme.

CAT: Yeah?

RIMMER: You thought it was all one film?

CAT: Sure – I thought it was a chilling morality tale about how some badly behaved ducks got turned into a couple of wailing human beings.

HOLLY: Hang on, chaps – I've got a blip. Quadrant four, sector four-niner-two.

KRYTEN: On my way, Holly.

KRYTEN *crosses to the cockpit.*

RIMMER: I'm sorry, but that kind of movie really irritates me. Totally unrealistic. There isn't a man in the universe who wouldn't have taken the job and to hell with the woman. Total baloney.

LISTER: Rimmer – that's what you said about *King of Kings*, the story of Jesus.

RIMMER: Well, it's true. A simple carpenter's son who learns how to do magic tricks like that and doesn't go into showbusiness? Do any of us believe that even for a second?

LISTER: He was supposed to be the Son of God.

RIMMER: I don't care. When he was carrying that cross up the hill, any normal, realistic bloke would have used it to clobber the guard on the left, mule-kicked the one on the right, and he'd have been over that green hill and down the other side before you could say 'Pontius Pilate'.

LISTER: Why do I feel you've missed the point? Whether you believe that stuff or not, it's about a dude who sacrificed his life for love. He wasn't interested in scarpering from his own crucifixion.

RIMMER: I don't buy it. Not realistic. As if!

LISTER: You've got no soul, man. No soul.

KRYTEN: (*Calls from cockpit*) Sirs, I think you should take a look at this.

3. Int. *Starbug* cockpit. Night

KRYTEN *is hunched over the radar as the others come in behind him.*

RIMMER: Another vessel?

LISTER: Too small . . . More like a missile.

KRYTEN: Impact in thirty-seven seconds.

HOLLY: Plotting random evasion course.

CAT: What? Am I the only sane one here? Why don't we lower the defensive shields?

KRYTEN: A superlative notion, sir, with only two tiny flaws: first, we don't have any defensive shields, and second: we don't have any defensive shields. I know technically speaking that's only one flaw, but I felt it was such a big one it was worth mentioning twice.

CAT: Good point, well made.

4. Model shot

A comet-like 'missile' heads for Starbug — *in fact it's a very bright, electronic blue light, with a tail.*

5. Int. *Starbug* cockpit. Night

We see over the CREW*'s shoulders as the light fills the windscreen and floods the cabin.*

6. Model shot

The 'missile' passes through Starbug*'s hull without damaging it.*

7. Int. *Starbug* cockpit. Night

The light-point shoots through the cockpit section and into the rear section.

8. Int. *Starbug* rear. Night

The CREW *appear in the doorway and cautiously walk down into the rear section as the light hovers around.* RIMMER *is somehow drawn towards it.*

LISTER: Rimmer – what are you doing?
RIMMER: Incredible . . . It's beautiful.

The light buzzes around RIMMER, *like the birds around Uncle Remus in* Song of the South.

KRYTEN: It's not registering on any scale . . . mass, velocity, molecular structure . . . all the readings are zero.

The light whooshes past them and out of the rear, through the cockpit section.

9. Int. *Starbug* cockpit. Night

We see through the windscreen as the CREW *run into the cockpit, the light streaking away into the middle distance. It stops.*

KRYTEN: (*Checking radar*) Ten thousand metres and holding . . .

10. Model shot

The light-point flares dramatically, and from it, an enormous, beautiful ship blooms into existence. It's covered in lights and almost transparent. This is the SSS Enlightenment.

11. Int. *Starbug* cockpit. Night
The CREW *bathed in light from the ship. They all shield their eyes and look out.*

KRYTEN: Sir — I'm picking up some kind of energy emission.

Suddenly RIMMER *is trapped in a beam of red light from over his head. He is sucked up into the light, and the light vanishes.*

KRYTEN: They've taken Rimmer! Sir — they've taken Rimmer.
CAT: Quick — let's get out of here before they bring him back.

12. Int. Holoship sleeping quarters
A fairly sumptuous, futuristic suite — officer quarters. The red light beam delivers RIMMER *into the room. Baffled he starts to wander about, trying to work out where he is. The door slides open, and an attractive but cool and no-nonsense female officer,* NIRVANA CRANE, *strides into the room.*

NIRVANA: I hope we didn't startle you. (*She shakes* RIMMER *by the hand*) Nirvana Crane.
RIMMER: You touched me.

She tosses RIMMER *a glass ornament. He catches it.*

RIMMER: I can touch . . . everything?

She pours them drinks from an odd futuristic container.

RIMMER: How is this possible?
NIRVANA: This entire ship, its crew, and everything on it is computer-generated.
RIMMER: You're all holograms? Even the ship?
NIRVANA: (*Clinks his glass*) Salut!
RIMMER: (*Grins*) Salut!

13. Int. Lift. Holoship. Day

RIMMER *and* NIRVANA *are in a futuristic lift – striplights up the side indicate lift movement.*

LIFT: Floor 124, Maintenance Department . . .

RIMMER: . . . but what's your mission?

NIRVANA: Exploration. We trawl deep space, in search of new life-forms and unique physical phenomena.

RIMMER: Fascinating. How big's the crew?

NIRVANA: Just under two thousand. All top flight personnel.

RIMMER: What a ship. What a magnificent vessel.

LIFT: Floor 125, Sports and Sexual Recreation.

RIMMER: Sports and what?

NIRVANA: Sex. Don't you have a Sex Deck on your ship?

RIMMER: No.

NIRVANA: Well, what do you do when you want to have sex?

RIMMER: Well, we go for runs . . . watch gardening pro-grammes on the ship's vid . . . play blow football . . . lots of things.

NIRVANA: That's . . . very bad for you. Don't you ever feel tense and frustrated?

RIMMER: Well, it's got worse these last ten years or so. I can't deny it. But uh . . .

NIRVANA: Extraordinary. It's quite different here. In fact it's a ship regulation that we all have sexual congress at least twice a day. It's a health rule.

RIMMER: Twice a day? That's more than some people manage in a lifetime!

He catches her expression – puzzled.

RIMMER: I mean, sad people. Sad, sad, lonely people. (*BEAT*) Whu-what happens if you don't have a partner?

NIRVANA: (*Not understanding*) If you don't have a partner?

RIMMER: I mean, some people . . . sad, lonely people . . . find that they're just . . . that people . . . that people just aren't attracted to them in . . . in that way.

NIRVANA: I don't understand. Here, it's considered the height of bad manners to refuse an offer of sexual coupling.

RIMMER: (*Pause.*) Well . . . people have always complimented me on my good manners . . . What a ship!

NIRVANA: We discarded the concept of family in the twenty-fifth century, when scientists finally proved that all our hang-ups and neuroses are caused by our parents.

RIMMER: I knew it!

NIRVANA: Families are disastrous for your mental health. So are relationships. These are outmoded concepts for us.

RIMMER: What about love? I mean, surely people still fall in love.

NIRVANA: We have developed beyond 'love', Mr Rimmer. It is a short-term hormonal distraction which interferes with the pure pursuit of personal advancement. We are holograms: there is no risk of disease or pregnancy. That's why, in our society, we only believe in sex. Constant, guilt-free sex.

RIMMER: Well, Nirvana, I always say: when in Rome . . . wear a toga.

Lift stops.

LIFT: Deck 177, Senior Officers' Quarters.

NIRVANA: Our floor. Come on, meet the Captain. Then if there's time, we'll grab some supper and have sex.

She walks out of the lift, leaving RIMMER *temporarily stunned. He gathers himself together.*

RIMMER: Oh, that would be lovely. (*Starts to follow her, out of shot*) Yes, lovely . . .

14. Int. *Starbug* cockpit. Gloomy

KRYTEN *and* LISTER *are bent over the monitors.*

KRYTEN: Poor Mr Rimmer. I fear he is in great danger.

HOLLY: I'm trying to get them to handshake, but they're not responding on any frequency.

CAT: Well, I say let's break out the laser cannons and give 'em both barrels.

KRYTEN: An adroit proposal, sir, with just two small drawbacks . . .

CAT: OK, forget it.

LISTER: There's nothing to shoot at. Look at the read-outs: zero mass.

KRYTEN: Of course – it's a holoship!

LISTER: A holoship?

KRYTEN: The project was in its initial phase when I left the solar system. Ships of no mass or volume, able to travel as superlight particles – tachyons – through wormholes and stargates. Crewed entirely by holograms of great genius and bravery.

LISTER: And they've taken Rimmer? He should fit in just perfectly.

KRYTEN: Now I understand why they didn't bother with a handshake: holocrews are legendarily arrogant. They despise stupidity wherever they see it, and they see it everywhere.

HOLLY: Hang on – I'm getting another energy emission . . .

15. Int. *Starbug* rear. Gloomy

The red light appears again and delivers a holoship officer, COM-MANDER BINKS: good-looking, well-built. He carries a psi-scan. The OTHERS step down from the cockpit.

BINKS: (*Looks around, snorts in amusement and activates communicator*) Binks to *Enlightenment*. I've arrived on the derelict.

He activates his scan, and ignores the CREW, treating them as if they were furniture.

BINKS: Confirm initial speculation: there is absolutely nothing of value or interest here.

Walks past them into the cockpit.

BINKS: It's one of the old class 2 ship-to-surface vessels. The very model, in fact, which was withdrawn due to major flight design flaws.

He steps back down into the rear and runs his scan over KRYTEN.

BINKS: Crew three: one series four thousand mechanoid: almost burnt out. Give it maybe three years. Nothing of salvageable value.

KRYTEN *and* LISTER *exchange looks.* BINKS *scans the* CAT.

BINKS: Ah, *felis sapiens.* Bred from the domestic house cat, and about half as smart. No value in future study of this species.

BINKS *scans* LISTER.

BINKS: What have we here? Rare fish indeed: a human being. Or a very close approximation. It's a live one. Chronological age: mid-twenties; physical age: approximately forty-seven. Grossly overweight. Unnecessarily ugly. Otherwise, I'd recommend it for the museum. Apart from that, of no value or interest.

LISTER *takes cigarette packet out of his pocket and pretends to scan* BINKS.

LISTER: Lister to *Red Dwarf.* We have in our midst a total smegpot. Brains in the anal region, chin absent, presumed missing. Genitalia small and inoffensive: of no value or interest.

BINKS: Binks to *Enlightenment*: evidence of primitive humour – the human displays knowledge of irony, satire and imitation. With patient tuition could maybe master simple tasks.

LISTER: Lister to *Red Dwarf.* Displays evidence of spoiling for a rumble. Seems unable to grasp simple threats. With careful pummelling could possibly be sucking tomorrow's lunch through a straw.

BINKS: Binks to *Enlightenment.* The human appears to be under the delusion that he is somehow able to bestow physical violence to a hologram. An amusingly common misconception in lower life-forms.

LISTER: Lister to *Red Dwarf.* The intruder appears to be blissfully unaware that we have a rather sturdy holo-whip in the munitions cabinet. And if he doesn't want his derrière minced like burger meat, he'd better be history in two seconds flat.

BINKS: Binks to *Enlightenment*. Recon mission complete. Transmit. (*BEAT*) With speed. (*BEAT*) *Enlightenment*. Quickly please.

And BINKS *is spirited away.*

16. Int. Holoship meeting room. Day

This is the captain's briefing room. The CAPTAIN, *behind his desk, is holding a briefing session with his* NUMBER TWO *(male) officer, who is seated.*

CAPTAIN: . . . So what you seem to be implying, Mr Navarro, is the wormhole may well be compacted.

NUMBER TWO: It's a remote possibility, sir.

CAPTAIN: But one we should consider . . .

NUMBER ONE *(female) enters and salutes.*

CAPTAIN: Ah, Commander. Any news?

NUMBER ONE: Yes, Captain — we're just getting the first-stage projections on the dimension probabilities of the stargate.

She hands the CAPTAIN *a perspex sheet, which he glances at.*

CAPTAIN: Interesting. Get them over to stochastic diagnostics, Mr Navarro, give me star charts for anything with a probability over point five.

NUMBER TWO: Aye, aye, sir.

NIRVANA *and* RIMMER *come in.*

NIRVANA: Captain, Mr Rimmer from the mining ship, *Red Dwarf*.

NIRVANA *leaves. The* CAPTAIN *crosses to a computer terminal downstage of* RIMMER, *sparing him but a glance.*

CAPTAIN: Mr Rimmer? My word – one of the old class-one holograms. I didn't think you fellows were still around. (*Shakes Rimmer's hand*.) Captain Hercules Platini, IQ 212. Number One . . .

NUMBER ONE: Commander Natalina Pushkin, IQ 201.

NUMBER TWO: Commander Randy Navarro, IQ 194.

RIMMER: Second Technician Arnold Rimmer, IQ unknown. This is an incredible ship, Captain.

CAPTAIN: So it should be, Mr Rimmer. After all, it's designed to carry the hologramatic cream of the Space Corps. Every member of this crew is the Top Gun of his or her field. This is a ship, Mr Rimmer, of superhumans.

RIMMER: Which is why, Captain, I feel I could really belong here.

NUMBER ONE: Are you serious?

RIMMER: Everything I want in my life is here on this ship. I want to join you.

CAPTAIN: But, Mr Rimmer – you're not an officer.

RIMMER: Captain, I've been in effective command of *Red Dwarf* for nearly four years now. I've guided that ragamuffin, ragtail crew of whacked-out crazies and hippy peaceniks through hell and back. The respect they feel for me doesn't come from badges on my chest or stripes on my sleeves. It was forged in the blue fire of combat. If I gave the order, those guys would crawl on their bellies across broken glass with their flies un-zipped. So don't tell me I'm not an officer, Captain, just because in deep space there's no Academy around to award me my pips. You've got to take me.

CAPTAIN: It's not quite that simple, Mr Rimmer – the *Enlightenment* already has a full ship's complement. The only way in is dead man's boots.

NUMBER ONE: You have to challenge an existing crew member. There are tests that tax the entire vista of your intellect.

RIMMER: Oh.

NUMBER TWO: Tests that probe every aspect of your mental capability.

RIMMER: Ah.

CAPTAIN: Should you win, your opponent's run-time would be terminated, and their life energy would be used to generate you.

RIMMER: They would be dead?

CAPTAIN: Mr Rimmer – we are *Übermensch*: there isn't a man, woman or cabbage on this ship who would fear a challenge from you.

RIMMER: Then I issue that challenge. Who will be my opponent?

CAPTAIN: Our computer will no doubt select the most stimulating match-up. It has stochastic capabilities.

RIMMER: Stochastic, eh? No kidding?

NUMBER ONE: (*Typing into a keyboard*.) It predicts the future with only a 5 per cent error margin, simply by extrapolating the most likely outcome of all known variables. I'm asking for your best chance of success. Here it is: your best shot is crew member 4172. You have a 96 per cent probability of failure.

CAPTAIN: (*To* NUMBER TWO) Mr Navarro, inform 4172 of the challenge. (*To* RIMMER) You have twenty-four hours to prepare, Mr Rimmer.

17. Int. Holoship corridor. Day

RIMMER *and* NIRVANA, *walking back to departure point.*

RIMMER: Well, Commander, thank you for a most fascinating afternoon. It's been most . . . fascinating.

NIRVANA: Perhaps, if you're not in any great rush, Mr Rimmer, we could retire to my quarters and have sex for a few hours?

RIMMER *looks at his watch.*

RIMMER: Well, I mean, uh . . . I had . . . (*Laughs*) Is that the time? God!

NIRVANA: Perhaps you find me unattractive?

RIMMER: Absolutely not, no. It's just . . . I had this thing to do, back on . . . (*indicates* Red Dwarf *with his thumb*) and, uh (*holds up his watch and taps it*), look, it's nearly half-past already, and, uuh . . . perhaps some other . . .

NIRVANA: Come . . . you need the exercise.

She takes his hand and leads him off.

RIMMER: Where are we going? (*She doesn't answer.*) Look, I'm not very good at this sort of thing. Well, as far as I know. I have experience of course, but, uh . . . Oh look, is that the table tennis room? I haven't played that in ages. Don't suppose you'd like a quick couple of sets . . .

But she leads him, meekly, off.

18. Model shot
Holoship in space. MIX TO:

19. Int. Nirvana's Quarters. Moody
RIMMER *and* NIRVANA *are lying post-coitally under silk sheets.*

RIMMER: That was just . . . unbelievable.

NIRVANA: Nobody's ever made love to me like that before.

RIMMER: Was it OK?

NIRVANA: It was . . . different.

RIMMER: Different?

NIRVANA: It had such . . . gusto.

RIMMER: It's probably coming from a large family. At mealtimes we always had to eat as fast as we could so we could get back for seconds.

NIRVANA: You make love like a Japanese meal – small portions, but so many courses.

RIMMER: Listen. I'm not very good at this sort of thing, but I just want to say . . . I think you are the most beautiful woman I've ever seen who didn't have staples through her stomach. Really, you're gorgeous, I mean, I'm constantly fighting the urge to fold you into thirds. Oh, God, what am I saying? Someone stop me. I'm trying to say you are incredibly incredible.

NIRVANA: That's not our way. We don't pay compliments. This is just . . . exercise. Nothing more.

RIMMER: That's all it is to me, too, too. Exercise. It's just . . . I've never worked out with such fantastic gym equipment.

NIRVANA: Emotion distracts the mind from the pursuit of intellectual excellence. We must dress and go now.

RIMMER: Look, Nirvana, what I'm trying to say is . . .

NIRVANA: Please don't say anything.

They both swing their legs over the edge of the bed (they are both in long T-shirts) so they are facing away from each other.

RIMMER: Look – I hope you didn't get the wrong idea, back there. It meant nothing to me. Really. Less than nothing. Truly.

NIRVANA: Good.

RIMMER: We might as well have been playing tennis.

NIRVANA: As it should be.

RIMMER: I, uh, I don't suppose you fancy a tie-break?

NIRVANA: I'm sorry. I've got things I should do.

RIMMER: Niet problemski.

Pregnant pause.

NIRVANA: You know, usually, we talk.

RIMMER: Talk?

NIRVANA: During the exercise.

RIMMER: What do you talk about?

NIRVANA: Ohh . . . research . . . new theories . . . mission profiles . . .

RIMMER: I'm sorry. I must have seemed very rude. I hardly said anything. Apart from 'Geronimo'.

She shakes his hand.

NIRVANA: Thank you for the work-out.

RIMMER: And thank you for what must rate as the weirdest afternoon of my life.

NIRVANA: Good luck with the challenge.

NIRVANA *looks at him a little too long.*

RIMMER: Dress!

TAPE STOP. RIMMER *is clothed.*

NIRVANA: Transmit.

RIMMER *vanishes.* NIRVANA *looks at her computer screen, which is flashing 'Message waiting'.*

NIRVANA: Privacy off.

NUMBER TWO *appears on screen.*

NUMBER TWO: (*VO, DIST*) Commander?
NIRVANA: Mr Navarro?
NUMBER TWO: Some amusing news – Stochy has chosen you to meet our guest's challenge.
NIRVANA: Me?
NUMBER TWO: (*VO, DIST*) Obviously it's ludicrous, but I do have to warn you officially that should you lose this challenge, you will lose your hologramatic status and be terminated. You have twenty-four hours to prepare.

NIRVANA *reacts.*

20. Model shot. *Red Dwarf* in space

21. Int. Sleeping quarters. Day
LISTER, CAT *and* KRYTEN, RIMMER *sitting around.*

KRYTEN: Well, this is absolutely wonderful news, sir, but if I may interject a note of caution: perhaps it's premature to get too excited. After all, your challenger will be a mental giant, a classifiable genius, and therefore it's just possible you may lose.
LISTER: May lose? Kryten, man – get real. He's got about as much chance as a Lil-let in an elephant.
RIMMER: I'm going to cheat.

KRYTEN: How can you cheat, sir? It's a contest of wits – your mind against his.

RIMMER: I'm not going to use my mind – I'm going to use somebody else's. Kryten, you're always saying humans only use 5 per cent of their brain's capacity.

KRYTEN: In some cases, much less.

RIMMER: (*Double take.*) That's 95 per cent left doing nothing. Look, we've got most of the ship's crew stored in the hologram library –

KRYTEN: Sir, what you're suggesting is immoral and illegal. Mind-patching is outlawed.

RIMMER: But it is possible.

KRYTEN: Possible, but highly dangerous. The side-effects can be devastating. You could be reduced to a gibbering simpleton.

CAT: Reduced?

RIMMER: I don't care – I'm prepared to take the chance.

LISTER: Even if it costs you your mind?

CAT: It's a small price to pay.

RIMMER: On that ship, I can touch, I can taste, I can feel. I'm not a half-man anymore: with them, I'm whole again.

LISTER: Rimmer, they're a bunch of arrogant, pompous, emotionally weird, stuck-up megalomaniacs. You really think you're ever going to fit in with them? (*BEAT*) What am I saying? *Bon voyage.*

KRYTEN: He's right, sir. Why d'you want to throw in with people like that?

RIMMER: Why? Because I want to be somebody, have a position of authority on a scout ship exploring uncharted space. Work alongside educated men and women, officers, people who count. This is my one chance to grab my dream, Lister, to be with the winners. Look at me. What do you see?

LISTER: Tell me.

RIMMER: You see a sad and lonely guy. A guy who left home at sixteen to become an officer and a gentleman, and ended up as a chicken soup machine-operative. Is it any wonder my father had four strokes? Is it any wonder he just used to sit at the window and dribble? I did that to him. Me.

LISTER: Look – there's nothing wrong with what you did. It was a job.

RIMMER: Have you ever seen a movie about a man in that job? Have you ever seen an adventure film about a guy who un-clogs vending machines? Did they ever make the film: *A Chicken Soup Machine-Operative and a Gentleman*? They didn't – and d'you know why? Because chicken soup machine-operatives are losers. And that's what I am.

LISTER: That's just your job.

RIMMER: You are your job.

KRYTEN: Not so, sir. Was Albert Camus a goalkeeper or a philosopher? Was Albert Einstein a clerk in a patent office or the greatest physicist who ever lived? And of course, there is the oft-told tale of the simple carpenter's son, who went on to own the largest chain of pizza stores in history – Harry Beedlebaum.

RIMMER: Albert Einstein didn't spend the best years of his life picking lumps of desiccated poultry from the end of his nozzle-cleaner.

LISTER: That doesn't make you a failure.

RIMMER: It does in my parents' eyes. It does in my brothers' eyes. It does in the eyes of everyone *with* eyes. That's exactly what it makes me.

KRYTEN: Sir, I implore you. Aside from the risk to your sanity, you're not even considering the moral implications. You will be joining a society where you'll be compelled to have sex with brilliant, beautiful women twice daily on demand. Am I the only one here who thinks that's just a little bit tacky? (*He looks around for support.*) Ah, well, clearly I am.

22. Int. Science room. Evening

RIMMER *is lying on a fluorescent slab. Suspended overhead is a perspex oblong, which can be positioned over the patient, and slid up and down his body. The surface of the oblong has keypad controls and several displays. (This is the MediBench – we'll be using it again.)* KRYTEN *is typing on to the MediBench.*

KRYTEN: Sir, I have uploaded the two candidates to share your mind. Science Officer Buchan – excellent scientific background, 169 IQ. And Flight-Co-ordinator McQueen – superlative mathematician, IQ 172. Even taking into account the enormous drag factor of your own mind, I still think we'll end up with something pretty special.

RIMMER: But I'll still have control.

KRYTEN: You will have access to their knowledge, but it'll be your personality that has overall control. But, sir, I implore you to reconsider. If not for yourself, then for that poor officer whose life you will take.

RIMMER: (*Sombre*) Wasn't it Saint Francis of Assisi himself who said: 'Never give a sucker an even break'?

KRYTEN: If he did, sir, it was strictly off the record.

RIMMER: Come on, get on with it.

KRYTEN: Commence download.

The machine starts to do things.

KRYTEN: In many ways, this is goodbye to Arnold Rimmer. Once these minds are enmeshed, there is no known way of extricating them. Effectively, this is your funeral. The personality we all know as Arnold J. Rimmer will cease to be.

RIMMER: And good riddance to the useless bastard, that's what I say.

KRYTEN *slides the perspex over* RIMMER*'s head.*

KRYTEN: Commencing integration.

The transformation begins.

RIMMER: Glory or insanity awaits!

23. Int. *Red Dwarf* corridor. Day
KRYTEN *and* LISTER *walking to the science room.*

LISTER: He's read every book in the medical library?

KRYTEN: It took him less than three hours. The change is quite astonishing.

They stop outside the science room door. KRYTEN *turns.*

KRYTEN: I must warn you, sir, this is not the useless pile of human wreckage we used to call 'Arnold Rimmer'. Prepare yourself.

24. Int. Science room. Day

RIMMER *is sitting, reading a computer screen. Pages of text flit across it at incredible speeds.* RIMMER *looks subtly different. His hair may be parted the other way, he sports tortoiseshell glasses, he has bad posture, and his body language is more professorial. Also, he has a strange snort when he finds things amusing.* KRYTEN *leans in.*

KRYTEN: Sir? We've received the transfer co-ordinates. We should be making tracks.

RIMMER: Kryten, I was just thinking . . . assuming, of course, that we are not dealing with five-dimensional objects, in a basically Euclidian geometric universe, and given the essential premise that all geomathematics are based on the hideously limiting notion that one plus one equals two, and not as Ustermayer correctly postulates, that one and two are in fact the same thing observed from different precepts, (*snort*) the theoretical shapes described by Sidis must be: a poly-dri-doc-dec-ahooey-hedron, a hexa-sexa-hedro-adecon and a di-bi-dolly-he-deca-dodron. Everything else is poppycock! Isn't that so?

LISTER: Rimmer . . .?

RIMMER: Yes, indeed, it is I. Or, since you colloquially prefer the accusative to the nominative: it is me. (*Snort, snort.*)

KRYTEN: Sir, we really should be . . . We don't want to miss the connection.

RIMMER *stands up and leads them into the corridor.*

RIMMER: Nonsense. Even by the most circuitous route, per-
ambulating briskly should achieve our objective in four point
three seven minutes . . .

25. Int. *Red Dwarf* corridor. Day
As they walk to the departure point:

RIMMER: I wrote a palindromic haiku this morning: perhaps
you'd like to hear it?
KRYTEN: I'm afraid we don't speak Japanese, sir.
RIMMER: I could translate it into Mandarin.
LISTER: Rimmer, we don't speak Japanese, we don't speak Mandarin and we don't speak Satsuma. (*To* KRYTEN) He's really
beginning to get on my pecs.
KRYTEN: Sir, you have to realize: he's operating on an entirely
different level from us, now. To him, we are the intellectual
equivalent of domestic science teachers.

They reach the spot in the cargo hold. RIMMER *stands in white circle.*
KRYTEN *speaks into the transmitter.*

KRYTEN: Subject ready for transfer. (*To* RIMMER) It's probably
spurious to wish you good luck.
RIMMER: It is indeed. Farewell, gentlemen – glory awaits.

And RIMMER *vanishes.*

26. PRE-VT. Int. Holoship quarters. Day
RIMMER *is seated at a desk. The two monitors, arranged in an 'L'
shape, each with a keyboard and a set of headphones. The monitors blink
into life, and the* CAPTAIN *addresses him from the screen:*

CAPTAIN: Attention, candidates. To preserve the pure intellectual nature of this challenge, you will remain in separate
suites. The questions will come through your headphones, in a
variety of different languages to confuse and disorient you.
There will be a total of two hundred thousand questions in

this initial session. When you have completed the tasks at workstation A, proceed to workstation B.

RIMMER *snorts and puts on both sets of headphones, arranging himself in between the two banks of monitors.*

RIMMER: I shall undertake both tasks simultaneously, if it's all the same to you.
CAPTAIN: That's impossible, Mr Rimmer.
RIMMER: None the less, I shall attempt it.
CAPTAIN: It begins.

We hear indecipherable babble distorted through each headset, as RIMMER, *Rick Wakeman-like, types simultaneously into both sets of keyboards.*

Music leads us into a quickish montage: intercut between RIMMER's *face, barely taxed; his running-score clocking up; Nirvana's lagging far behind; his fingers dancing across keyboards; the word 'Correct' flashing on screen, rapidly; a couple of shots of Nirvana in similar quarters, typing away steadily. The montage ends with the screens scrolling up verbose answers.*

Suddenly the answers are gibberish. We cut to RIMMER's *face: it's twitching uncontrollably. He takes off his glasses, rubs his eyes, and drags his hands through his hair. From the look on his face, we realize that normal* RIMMER *is coming back. A few more twitches and* RIMMER *the genius returns. He snorts and starts typing maniacally. A series of more violent twitches and* RIMMER's *back again, this time for good. He tries typing with one finger and looks sad. We see his opponent's score rapidly catching up with his own now static score.* RIMMER *closes his eyes in desperate exasperation.*

27. Model shot. *Red Dwarf* in space
MIX TO:

28. Int. *Red Dwarf* corridor. Evening
Rimmer appears in mid-flight, racing along. He skids into:

29. Int. Science room. Evening

Empty. HOLLY *on screen looking vacant.*

RIMMER: Kryten – where is he?

HOLLY: 'Hello, Holly, how are you?' 'Fine thanks, Arnold.' 'You haven't seen Kryten, have you?' 'I have, actually, he's in the sleeping quarters . . .'

RIMMER *races out.*

HOLLY: . . . 'Thanks a lot, Hol.' 'Not at all, Arn. See you.' ''Bye.' What a charming man.

30. Int. Sleeping quarters. Evening

SHOT: HARRISON, *a woman in* Red Dwarf *hologram uniform with 'H' on her forehead.* HOLLY *is on the screen.*

HARRISON: . . . cinema, literature, the theatre, horse-riding and ballet . . . and that's about it.

We see LISTER, *the* CAT *and* KRYTEN *are interviewing.*

LISTER: Well, that's terrific, uh, Chantel. You sound exactly what we're looking for. Are there any questions you want to ask us?

HARRISON: I just want to get this clear in my mind: this is an opportunity to be revived as a hologram and become a part of the crew. And the crew is you three.

They smile winningly.

HARRISON: Basically, you spend your time salvaging derelict spaceships, playing poker and eating curries.

LISTER: Well, we don't do that much salvaging.

HARRISON: But you sound like you eat a lot of curries.

KRYTEN: Well, it's not curries absolutely every night, if that's what you mean. Why, only last June, I remember quite distinctly Mr Lister had a pizza. (*To* LISTER) Remember? And you didn't like it until I poured some curry sauce on it, and then you just yummed it up.

HARRISON: And the all-night poker sessions: is it always strip poker?

LISTER: Well, that depends how drunk we are.

CAT: Or how much curry he's had.

HARRISON: So, this probably sounds like a stupid question: you don't really have much interest in horse-riding or ballet?

LISTER: Yeah. Sure. Absolutely. So long as we can go for a curry afterwards, we're cool. So, obviously, there's a couple of other people to see, but in theory, would you be interested if we offered you the position as replacement hologram?

HARRISON: No.

LISTER: No.

HARRISON: No. I think . . . uhm . . . I'm better off where I am.

CAT: But you're dead!

HARRISON: Right. And meeting you guys has really made me appreciate it a whole lot more.

KRYTEN: Well, uh, thank you very much Ms Harrison. Uh. Thank you.

LISTER: Next.

And HARRISON *vanishes.*

HOLLY: Uploading the next candidate.

LISTER: So. Is any kind of favourite emerging?

CAT: There's a certain pattern emerging which is hard to ignore.

KRYTEN: He's right, sir. All of the candidates who could loosely be described as 'desirable' either make weak excuses or say 'no'. Indeed, so far we have only one acceptance, and that was from your own hologram, sir.

LISTER: Well. Two of me maybe wouldn't be so terrible.

CAT: I think we can do better.

LISTER: What's wrong with having two of me?

CAT: Well, first let's address the problem of what's wrong with having *one* of you.

A shimmering figure begins to appear.

HOLLY: Next candidate. Deck-Sergeant Sam Murray.

SAM MURRAY *appears, complete with 'H'.*

LISTER: Sam, as Holly's told you –

RIMMER *runs in.*

RIMMER: Kryten! My own mind's come back – you've got to help me.

KRYTEN: What happened exactly? Was there a gradual deterioration in your intelligence, or did it happen within seconds?

RIMMER: Seconds! Come on – I'm in the middle of the assessment – you've got to give me another mind-patch, pronto.

KRYTEN: I'm sorry sir, it's classic rejection syndrome. If the minds have unmeshed, there's nothing we can do about it.

RIMMER: What are you talking about?

KRYTEN: It means you don't have the kind of brain that can cope with implants.

RIMMER: No! No!

KRYTEN: I'm sorry, sir.

RIMMER: There must be some way . . .

KRYTEN: I'm afraid not.

RIMMER: But I'm winning! I'm so close . . . (*Notices* MURRAY *for the first time.*) Who's this?

Everyone counts their shoelaces.

RIMMER: My God. You're choosing my replacement! I'm not even gone, and you're choosing my replacement.

LISTER: We thought you weren't coming back.

RIMMER: Well, you should have known better. You expect something to actually go right, for me? Arnold Schmucko Rimmer? Tosspot by Royal Appointment?

RIMMER *turns to go.*

KRYTEN: Where are you going?

RIMMER: I'm going to withdraw.

31. Model shot. Holoship in space

32. Int. Holoship lift. Night

RIMMER, *forlorn and bitter, leaning against the lift wall.* NUMBER ONE *is in the lift. She smiles.*

NUMBER ONE: Hi.

RIMMER: (*Grunts.*)

NUMBER ONE: I hear you're doing really well in the assessment.

RIMMER: (*Grunts.*)

NUMBER ONE: Well, listen, if you make it through, maybe we could have sex sometime next week. I'm free Wednesday morning.

RIMMER: I'm sorry, I'm busy Wednesday. I'm killing myself.

Lift doors open and NUMBER ONE *leaves.* NIRVANA *gets in.*

NIRVANA: Arnie, where've you been?

RIMMER: To hell and back. I'm withdrawing from the challenge.

NIRVANA: But you're winning.

RIMMER: I was using a mind-patch. It's all gone wrong. Oh, God . . .

NIRVANA: A mind-patch? Are you insane?

RIMMER: No. I'd have done anything. Anything to get on this ship. I'd have happily inserted red hot needles through both my ears and tap-danced the title song from *42nd Street* barefoot on a bed of molten lava while simultaneously giving oral sex to a male orang-utan with dubious personal hygiene if only I could have got a post on this vessel.

NIRVANA: Why do you want it so badly?

RIMMER: Every time I look in the mirror I see this (*taps 'H'*). Only, to me it doesn't stand for 'Hologram', it stands for 'Hopeless', 'Half-wit', 'Hideous failure'. This was a chance to be somebody. Somebody I liked.

NIRVANA *looks at him. There is tenderness in her face.*

NIRVANA: I've never met anyone like you before.

RIMMER: Everyone says that.

NIRVANA: Listen to me, mister: underneath all that neurotic mess is someone nice trying to get out.

RIMMER *looks round. Is she talking about him?*

NIRVANA: Someone who deserves a chance to grow. So you won't give up, OK? OK?

RIMMER: I cheated . . .

NIRVANA: You're going to win, Arnie. You're going to get your dream. I promise you.

RIMMER: You really think?

NIRVANA: (*Smiles, kisses her finger and presses it to* RIMMER's *lips.*) I really think.

33. Model shot. *Red Dwarf* in space, by the Holoship

34. Int. *Red Dwarf* corridor. Evening

RIMMER *materializes and starts to walk down the corridor. He looks . . . distracted.*

35. Int. Sleeping quarters. Evening

LISTER *and the* CAT *playing cards.* RIMMER *walks in. They look up.*

RIMMER: (*Quietly*) I won.

LISTER: What?

RIMMER: My opponent withdrew. I won. I'm an officer. I leave tonight.

36. Int. Cargo bay area. Night

RIMMER, *looking splendid in full SSS* Enlightenment *officer uniform walking towards the departure point, followed by* LISTER, KRYTEN *and the* CAT. *Holly is on a monitor.*

RIMMER: I'm not much at big speeches, and I know I haven't always been an easy guy to get on with. And if I'd been given the choice, I admit, I probably wouldn't have chosen you as friends. Circumstances flung us together, but over the years, I've come to regard you as . . . people . . . I've met.

LISTER: You're breaking me up, Rimmer.

RIMMER: Well. Better get going.

LISTER: See you, smeghead.

RIMMER: Yeah.

RIMMER *nods at* KRYTEN.

KRYTEN: (*Into communicator*) Transfer.

RIMMER *vanishes.*

37. Int. Holoship quarters. Night

Nirvana's quarters. NUMBER TWO *is showing* RIMMER *in.*

NUMBER TWO: And these are your quarters, Mr Rimmer.

RIMMER: There must be some error. These are Commander Crane's quarters.

NUMBER TWO: Didn't you know? She was your opponent.

SHOT: RIMMER's *face falls apart as he realizes what she's done.*

38. Int. Captain's quarters. Night

The CAPTAIN *is bent over some data with* NUMBER ONE. RIMMER *walks up to the* CAPTAIN *and salutes (properly).*

RIMMER: Navigation Officer Rimmer reporting. Permission to speak, sir.

CAPTAIN: Mr Rimmer. Welcome aboard. I trust everything's –

RIMMER: I wish to resign my commission, sir.

CAPTAIN: Resign? May I ask your reasoning, Mr Rimmer?

RIMMER: Flight-Commander Crane has taken leave of her senses and fallen in love with me, sir.

CAPTAIN: Love? Surely not. Commander Crane is far too intellectually advanced to submit to a mere short-term hormonal imbalance, Mr Rimmer.

RIMMER: That's why she withdrew from the challenge and allowed me to win.

CAPTAIN: Mr Rimmer, what you're suggesting is that she cared more for your happiness than she did her own life.

RIMMER: Am I? Yes, sir, I suppose I am, sir.

CAPTAIN: And now you're doing something equally unfathomable: resigning, so she can be reinstated. Even though here you could have everything: an effective physical presence, a position of command, everything.

RIMMER: (*Hands over envelope*) Perhaps you'll be kind enough to pass on this note to her.

CAPTAIN: I understand the gesture, Mr Rimmer, but your resignation solves nothing. After all, the two of you will still be apart.

RIMMER: Permission to return to *Red Dwarf*, sir.

CAPTAIN: Granted.

RIMMER *turns to go.*

RIMMER: And you're wrong, sir. We won't be apart. We . . . just won't be together. (*Long pause.*) I cannot believe I said that.

He turns to go, and we:

Run credits

CAMILLE

1. Int. Sleeping quarters. Day

LISTER *at the table, opposite* KRYTEN. LISTER *puts a banana on the table.*

LISTER: OK, try again: what's this?

KRYTEN: It's a banana.

LISTER: No! Try again. What is it?

KRYTEN: It's a banana!

LISTER: No it isn't – what is it?

KRYTEN: It's an orhh ... it's an orrrhhhhn ... it's an orrrrrrrrrrrrr ...

LISTER: Orange. Go on, say it: it's an orange. This is an orange.

KRYTEN: It's an ornononhhguh ... it's a nuuuuuggggh ... it's a banana. I'm sorry, sir, I just can't do it.

LISTER: You can do it – I'm going to teach you how to do it. What's this?

Replaces banana with apple.

KRYTEN: It's an app–

LISTER: No! What is it?

KRYTEN: I'm sorry, sir, I just can't lie! I'm programmed always to tell the truth.

LISTER: It's easy. Look. (*Holds up an apple*) An orange. (*Holds up orange*) A melon. (*Holds up banana*) A female aardvark.

KRYTEN: That's just so superb! How do you do that? Especially calling a banana an aardvark – an aardvark isn't even a fruit! That's total genius.

LISTER: Let's start again.

KRYTEN: Sir, my head is spinning, we've been doing this all morning.

LISTER: Kryten, I'm going to teach you how to lie and cheat if it's the last thing I do. I'm going to teach you how to be selfish, cruel and sarcastic – it's the only way to break your programming, make you independent.

KRYTEN: And I'm truly grateful, sir. Don't you think I'd love to be deceitful, unpleasant and offensive? Those are the human qualities I admire most. But I just can't do it!

LISTER: You can!

KRYTEN: I can't!

LISTER: (*Slams banana on table*) What's this!

KRYTEN: No!

LISTER: What is it?!

KRYTEN: Please!

LISTER: What is it?!

KRYTEN: It's a small off-duty Czechoslovakian traffic warden!

LISTER: Yes! What's this?

Puts apple on the table.

KRYTEN: It's a blue and red striped golfing-umbrella!

LISTER: Yes! And this?

Slams down orange.

KRYTEN: It's an orange!

LISTER: No – try again.

KRYTEN: It's the Bolivian navy on manoeuvres in the South Pacific.

LISTER: Hey, guy – you've got it.

KRYTEN: No, I haven't.

LISTER: Yes, you – (*realizes* KRYTEN*'s lied*) nice one.

KRYTEN: Well, I can't hang around here, I've got to take the penguin for a walk. I did it again! I can do it! I can lie!

CAT *comes in.*

LISTER: Hey, Cat, look at this.

CAT: Look at what?

LISTER *puts banana down on the table.*

LISTER: Kryten, what's this?

KRYTEN: It's a banana.

LISTER: (*Puts orange down on table*) What's this?

KRYTEN: It's an orange.

LISTER: (*Puts down apple*) This?

KRYTEN: An apple.

CAT: You taught him that? That's terrific. You two should audition for *What's My Fruit*.

LISTER: No, man. He didn't do it right.

CAT: It gets better?

KRYTEN: I can't do it, sir.

LISTER: You just did.

KRYTEN: I can't do it – not when someone else is there. What's a suitable human analogy? It's like trying to urinate in a public lavatory next to a man who's two feet taller than you. It's just not possible.

CAT: What are you trying to do, exactly?

KRYTEN: He's trying to teach me to lie, sir.

CAT: Any particular reason?

LISTER: Lying's a vital part of your psychological defence system. Without it, you're naked. If you can't lie, you can never conceal your intentions from other people. Sometimes that's essential. Like Nelson, when he put the telescope to his blind eye and said, 'I see no ships', or Bogart at the end of *Casablanca*, where he lies to Victor Laszlo to protect his feelings.

KRYTEN: And I understand the theory. How many times have you made me watch that movie? I understand that lying can be noble. I just can't do it!

LISTER: We try again. (*Holds up banana*) What's this?

KRYTEN: It's a banana! It's always been a banana, and it will always be a banana. It's a yellow fruit you unzip and eat the white bits. It's a banana!

RIMMER *comes on the vid screen.*

RIMMER: Lister, have you got Kryten there with you?

LISTER: Yeah. What's the prob?

RIMMER: The problem is: I've been waiting fully twenty-five minutes for him in the hangar.

KRYTEN: (*Curses*) Oh, spin my nipple nuts and send me to Alaska! I'm supposed to take him asteroid spotting. (*To screen*) I'll be right down, sir.

RIMMER: You'd better be.

Screen blanks.

LISTER: Remember yesterday's class – introduction to insults.

KRYTEN: Sir, I'm not ready yet.

LISTER: So, how do we address the gentleman who's just been on that screen?

KRYTEN: We call him Mr –

LISTER: No! Remember what we talked about. What is he?

KRYTEN: He's a . . . smerrrrrh . . . a smaaaaarrhhh . . .

LISTER: Come on, you can do it.

KRYTEN: He's a smoooorh . . . he's a smeeeeeeh . . .

LISTER: Nearly . . . nearly.

LISTER *takes out printed cards and holds up first one: it reads 'Smeg'.*

KRYTEN: He's a sme-e-egg . . .

LISTER *holds up second card: it reads 'Head'.*

KRYTEN: . . . he-e-a-add. I did it!

LISTER: Brutal. Now – the real test: can you say it to him in person?

2. Int. Hangar. Day

RIMMER *standing, impatiently looking at his watch.* KRYTEN *comes up.*

RIMMER: Ah! Kryten! At last. So glad you could make it this millennium.

KRYTEN: Smurrrrrrrrrr . . .

RIMMER: What?

KRYTEN: You're a smuuuurhhhhh . . . heeeeeee . . .

RIMMER: Pardon?

KRYTEN: Smerhhhhhhh . . . huaaaaaa . . . Oh, forget it.

3. Model shot. *Starbug* taking off
MIX TO:

4. Model shot. *Starbug* in space

5. Int. *Starbug* cockpit. Day
KRYTEN *is driving.* RIMMER *beside him.*

RIMMER: What a productive day. Barely nine hours in space, and we managed to spot two hundred and forty-nine asteroids. Marvellous.

HOLLY: Oh yeah, Big Chief I Spy'll be well pleased. You'll probably get a special little badge for this day's work.

RIMMER: (*Sneers at* HOLLY) Kryten, is there any possibility that we could go just a little bit faster? I mean, just so we're not being overtaken by stationary objects?

KRYTEN: Sir, you're a shmurrrrr . . .

RIMMER: A shmurr?

KRYTEN: A shmurrr-hurrrrr.

RIMMER: A shmurr-hurrr?

KRYTEN: A complete and total one.

HOLLY: Hang about. I'm picking something up. Some kind of distress beacon.

KRYTEN: (*Peering at controls*) I copy that, Holly. Quadrant four-niner-seven.

RIMMER: What is it?

HOLLY: Hard to tell. Whatever it is, it appears to be marooned on a planet in decaying orbit.

RIMMER: What's the safety margin?

HOLLY: The planet'll explode in about two hours.

RIMMER: Forget it – it's too dangerous. Head for home, Kryten.

KRYTEN: We can't just leave them there – there may be survivors.

RIMMER: Leave it, Kryten. That's an order.

KRYTEN *taps the controls and yanks the steering-column.*

RIMMER: What are you doing?

KRYTEN: I'm not plotting a course, sir, and I'm not taking her down.

RIMMER: Yes you are!

KRYTEN: Neither am I rendezvous-ing with the crashed vessel, nor am I seeking out survivors.

RIMMER: You're committing an act of mutiny. I could have you dismantled for this.

KRYTEN: Smeg-hurrrrrrrrrrh! Damn my programming!

6. Model shot. *Red Dwarf* in space

7. Int. Sleeping quarters. Day

LISTER *is watching the TV (we can't see the screen).* CAT *comes in.*

LISTER: They're not back yet? They've been hours.

CAT: No sign. What you watching?

LISTER: Oh, just a vid. It's a classic, man.

CAT: What is it?

LISTER: *Tales of the Riverbank – The Next Generation.*

CAT: Oh, right, I've seen this. It's not as good as the original.

LISTER: Well, they never really found anyone to replace Hammy Hamster.

CAT: How could they? The dude was a diva. He smouldered. The camera loved him.

LISTER: He was the rodent equivalent of Marlon Brando.

CAT: Wonder what happened to old Hammy? One minute he's a huge star, with his own gold wheel and as much cheese as he can hold in his cheeks – the next, obscurity.

LISTER: Probably went on the slide. Series ended, couldn't get any more work. Then, the ultimate humiliation – hamstergrams.

RIMMER *appears on the screen.*

RIMMER: Well, thanks a bunch, thanks a buncherooni.

LISTER: Rimmer. Where are you?

RIMMER: That idiot of a droid has endangered the entire vessel by landing on a planet that's about to explode, thanks to your foundation course in advanced rebellion.

LISTER: Why?

RIMMER: So he can go off and search some kind of starship escape vessel, because there's a million-to-one chance there may be a survivor.

LISTER: You let him go on his own?

RIMMER: Certainly I let him go on his own. I was glad to get rid of him. He's flipped. He's got mad droid disease. He kept waving a banana in my face and calling it a female aardvark.

LISTER: Well, you'd better get after him, he may need some help.

RIMMER: Look, it's pointless us both going off and getting terrorized to death by some deranged rampaging mutant. Much better if one of us stays here and survives to enjoy the full pleasure of being blown to smithereens in seventeen minutes' time. Where the smeg is he?

8. Int. *Penhalagen* corridor. Dark

KRYTEN *wandering along with bazookoid, holding torch.*

KRYTEN: Hello? Is anyone there? Can anyone read me?

9. Int. Gantry aboard *Penhalagen*. Dark

KRYTEN *with bazookoid is nervously looking around. We see some of the gantry give way under his feet. The gun tumbles a long way to the ground.* KRYTEN *is dangling by his fingertips.*

KRYTEN: (*Calls out*) Mr Rimmer, sir! Hello!

His voice echoes.

KRYTEN: (*Calls*) Can you hear me, sir? Help! Mr Rimmer?

SHOT: KRYTEN*'s face. We hear the sound of footsteps on metal.*

KRYTEN: Sir? Is that you, sir?

We hear a woman's voice:

CAMILLE: Give me your hand.

KRYTEN *lets go with his left hand, and holds it out. It is grabbed by another, identical, mechanoid hand, and he's hauled up. He is facing a* MECHANOID WOMAN. *The two mechanoids stand there, looking at one another.*

KRYTEN: Well, hello. I thank you from the bottom of my re-hydration unit. You saved my life.

MECHANOID CAMILLE: You responded to my distress call – you saved mine.

KRYTEN: My name is Kryten.

MECHANOID CAMILLE: They call me Camille. Pleased to make your acquaintance.

KRYTEN: Are you a 4000 series?

MECHANOID CAMILLE: Yes. I'm the 4000 series GTi.

KRYTEN: GTi? Oh, wow! I'm just a plain old 4000. You've got all the luxury extras, like realistic toes, and slide-back sun roof head . . . why are you looking at me that way? Is there something wrong?

MECHANOID CAMILLE: Sorry. Stare mode – cancel. It's just, you have really amazing eyes.

KRYTEN: (*Nervous*) Well, ahm, yes, they're the 579s with the automatic 15f stop cornea. If you like, I could pop them out, and you could borrow them. Oh, heck – what a jerky thing to say.

69

MECHANOID CAMILLE: I don't believe you could ever say anything which I would consider 'jerky'.

KRYTEN: Really?

MECHANOID CAMILLE: Really.

KRYTEN: Wow. (*Pause.*) Listen: I know this sounds like a corny line, but: has anyone ever told you the configuration and juxtaposition of your features is extraordinarily apposite?

She slaps his shoulder, playfully embarrassed.

MECHANOID CAMILLE: You really know all the lines, don't you?

KRYTEN: No, I mean it. The way the light catches the angles on your head, it's enchanting! (*Holds out his hand again*) I'm Kryten.

MECHANOID CAMILLE: You already said.

KRYTEN: I did? Oh yes. Gosh, you must think me as stupid as a photocopier. So, what happened here? Where are the crew?

MECHANOID CAMILLE: Kryten, do you believe in advanced mutual compatibility on the basis of a primary initial ident?

KRYTEN: You mean what humans call 'love at first sight'?

MECHANOID CAMILLE: That would be an adequate synonym, yes.

KRYTEN: Up until five minutes ago, I would have said it had a probability of zero squared.

MECHANOID CAMILLE: And now?

KRYTEN: This gantry is unstable. It might be wise if you hung on to me.

They link arms.

KRYTEN: What is that fragrance? It smells divine.

MECHANOID CAMILLE: WD40.

KRYTEN: That's what I thought! I use that on my neck hinges, too.

MECHANOID CAMILLE: Oh, Kryten, this shouldn't be happening. Do you feel it, too?

KRYTEN: You mean the 93.72 per cent compatibility factor?

MECHANOID CAMILLE: I make it 93.75.

Brett Riverboat and the Riviera Kid
Gunmen of the Apocalypse. Photo: Oliver Upton
'The answer's in these guns somehow'
Gunmen of the Apocalypse. Photo: Oliver Upton

(opposite) 'We won't be apart. We . . . just won't be together'
Holoship. Photo: Mike Vaughan
(above) 'Permission to return to *Red Dwarf*, sir'
Holoship. Photo: Mike Vaughan
(below) '*Salut!*'
Holoship. Photo: Mike Vaughan

(above) 'Everyone who looks at her perceives her differently'
Camille. Photo: Mike Vaughan
(below) 'From now on, my darling, *Casablanca* will be our movie . . .'
Camille. Photo: Mike Vaughan
(opposite) 'I think I E5, A9, B8, O7, you'
Camille. Photo: Mike Vaughan

'We are the Sensational Reverse Brothers'
Backwards. Photo: Paul Grant
'Thanks for your support'
Backwards. Photo: Paul Grant

(above) 'I think that little blonde one's giving you the eye'
Kryten. Photo courtesy of Grant Naylor Productions Ltd

(left) 'Miss Tracy . . . you look absolutely perfect'
Kryten. Photo courtesy of Grant Naylor Productions Ltd

(right) 'It's rather good, isn't it?'
Kryten. Photo courtesy of Grant Naylor Productions Ltd

(above) **'That little bit extra. That's what it's all about'**
Me². Photo courtesy of Grant Naylor Productions Ltd

(left) **'Souper'**
Me². Photo courtesy of Grant Naylor Productions Ltd

(below) **'It's no wonder Father never loved you'**
Me². Photo courtesy of Grant Naylor Productions Ltd

KRYTEN: Oh, that's right. I forgot to carry the three.

MECHANOID CAMILLE: Then say it. I want to hear the words.

KRYTEN: I can't – they sound so ridiculous coming from a mechanoid.

MECHANOID CAMILLE: Then say them in machine language.

KRYTEN: OK. In Z8 zero zero one two, using hex rather than binary, and converting to a basic ASC two code: Camille, I think I E5, A9, B8, O7 you.

MECHANOID CAMILLE: You really mean that?

KRYTEN: Camille, I'd do anything for you. I'd compute a three million digit prime number, with prime roots if I thought it would make you happy. I'd evaluate pi to infinity if it would make you smile.

MECHANOID CAMILLE: Oh, Kryten – you make the most romantic calculations.

Suddenly Kryten's walkie-talkie bursts into life.

RIMMER: (*VO, DIST*) Kryten? Can you read me? What's happening?

KRYTEN *reaches for his radio – Camille's hand stops him.*

MECHANOID CAMILLE: There are others?

KRYTEN: Yes – is something wrong?

MECHANOID CAMILLE: I can't meet them.

KRYTEN: What d'you mean?

MECHANOID CAMILLE: It would wreck everything. The two of us alone – we could make that work. Please don't ask me to explain . . .

KRYTEN: But, Camille, this entire planet is about to blow. There's no time . . .

MECHANOID CAMILLE: Please – I can't meet your shipmates – trust me.

KRYTEN *then reaches for his radio.*

KRYTEN: You don't know them, Camille – you'll like them. (*BEAT*) Well, some of them. (*BEAT*) Well, one of them.

(*BEAT*) Maybe. (*Into radio*) Sir, I'm making my way back.

RIMMER: (*VO, DIST*) What's kept you?

KRYTEN: I found a survivor, sir. We're coming in.

10. Int. *Starbug* rear section. Day

KRYTEN *comes in holding* MECHANOID CAMILLE *by the hand*.

MECHANOID CAMILLE: Kryten, please, don't make me do this – I'm begging you.

KRYTEN: Just relax, everything's going to be fine. (*Calls*) Mr Rimmer, sir.

RIMMER: Where the smeg have you been?

RIMMER *appears on the top of the steps from the cockpit*.

KRYTEN: Sir, I'd like you to meet Camille. Camille, this is Second Tech Rimmer. She saved my life, sir.

SHOT: RIMMER*'s reaction*.

RIMMER: Yes . . . well . . . howdy.

From Rimmer's POV: we see KRYTEN *is standing next to a* FEMALE HOLOGRAM *version of Camille (a different actress)*.

HOLOGRAM CAMILLE: Howdy.

TWO-SHOT: we see Camille as the MECHANOID *again*.

KRYTEN: You see? I knew you'd get along. Didn't I tell you? Well. We haven't got long. I'd better start up the engines and get us out of the impact zone.

MECHANOID CAMILLE: I'll come with you.

KRYTEN: No, no. You stay back here and get acquainted.

SHOT: RIMMER. *And* CAMILLE *is the hologram again*.

HOLOGRAM CAMILLE: Fine.

KRYTEN *goes to the cockpit section*. RIMMER *stands there. Embarrassed, as usual, in front of a woman*.

RIMMER: Can I get you anything, or anything?

HOLOGRAM CAMILLE: No. No, I'm fine, thanks.

RIMMER: I can't believe I've met another hologram after all these years.

HOLOGRAM CAMILLE: Yes, I was second technician aboard that crate . . .

RIMMER: Second technician! That's what I am.

HOLOGRAM CAMILLE: I always wanted to go further, but I'm a real dope when it comes to exams.

RIMMER: Me too!

HOLOGRAM CAMILLE: So. What do they call you?

RIMMER: Well, my first name's Arnold, but the guys generally just call me . . . (*looks around nervously*) 'Duke'.

HOLOGRAM CAMILLE: 'Duke'?

RIMMER: Yes, well they don't call me 'Duke' absolutely all the time. In fact, sometimes months can elapse, and they won't call me 'Duke' at all. So, don't call me 'Duke' in front of anyone, because they might have forgotten. You know, that they call me 'Duke'. Sorry, I'm blabbering. I'm not very good at small talk.

HOLOGRAM CAMILLE: I think you're perfectly charming.

RIMMER: Do you? Well, thank you. No one's ever said I was charming before. They've said, 'Rimmer, you're a total git,' but never 'charming', no.

HOLOGRAM CAMILLE: Well, I think you're very charming.

RIMMER: Really?

HOLOGRAM CAMILLE: Very, very charming.

RIMMER: Well, uh, thank you. Uhm, thank you. I'd better just check everything's OK with, uh, Kryten. *Excusez-moi.*

RIMMER *swaggers boldly into the cockpit section.*

11. Int. *Starbug* cockpit. Day

KRYTEN *is driving.* RIMMER *comes in and sits in the co-pilot seat. They both turn and grin at one another. As they refer to Camille, they look to the rear section, where the appropriate woman is seated.*

KRYTEN: She's quite something, isn't she, sir?

RIMMER: She's enchanting.

KRYTEN: You think so?

RIMMER: She's got everything: style, taste, poise. She's absolutely lovely.

KRYTEN: I'm so happy you think so, sir. I don't mind telling you: I think there's romance in the air.

RIMMER: You sly old dog, Krytie. I think you're right.

KRYTEN: Oh, sure, her nose is a little loose, but to me, that's just cute.

RIMMER *looks at him oddly.*

RIMMER: Are you feeling OK?

KRYTEN: Absolutely, sir.

RIMMER: I'll tell you something: she's so like my sister-in-law, Janine, it's untrue.

KRYTEN: Camille looks like your sister-in-law? What happened? Was she involved in some kind of horrific car accident?

RIMMER: Who? Janine? No, of course not. She was a model.

KRYTEN: And she looked like Camille?

RIMMER: Absolutely. The resemblance is uncanny.

KRYTEN: What did she model? Spark plugs?

RIMMER *looks at him oddly.*

RIMMER: I happen to think she's very attractive.

KRYTEN: You do?

RIMMER: Yes. Certainly.

KRYTEN *looks at* RIMMER *oddly.*

KRYTEN: Do you think *I'm* attractive?

RIMMER: You? Of course not. I think you look like a giant half-chewed rubber-tipped pencil.

KRYTEN: Well, you may think what the heck you like, sir. But there are other people in this big wide cosmos who happen to think I look pretty amazing. Especially in the eye department. I thank you so very much.

12. Model shot. *Starbug* **landing in hangar**
MIX TO:

13. Int. Medical unit. Day

MECHANOID CAMILLE *is on the MediBench.* KRYTEN *is tending her.* LISTER *comes in, swigging a can of lager.*

LISTER: You're back – I just heard.
KRYTEN: Ah, sir, you haven't met our visitor. Camille . . .

SHOT: KOCHANSKI-TYPE CAMILLE.

CAMILLE KOCHANSKI: Hi.
KRYTEN: Well, if you'll excuse me, I'll go and prepare your quarters. The penthouse suite on A-deck should suffice.

KRYTEN *goes.* LISTER *picks up clip-board with medical data on it.*

LISTER: Yep. Well. This looks fine. If you'd just like to remove your clothing, we'll begin the examination. (*Holds out his hand*) Sorry, Dave Lister, ship's surgeon.
CAMILLE KOCHANSKI: You're a surgeon?
LISTER: Well, I'm not fully qualified, but I have seen every episode of *St Elsewhere*. Still, if it makes you feel uncomfortable, we can completely dispense with the physical examination, and go straight for the malpractice. So, if you'd like to lie there and relax, I'll go and connect up the laughing gas. D'you want sniggers or guffaws? – It's all the same to me.
CAMILLE KOCHANSKI: Call me crazy, but something tells me you're not a doctor.
LISTER: What gave it away? The fact that I can go for more than ten seconds without patronizing you? Isn't this incredible? The last two human beings in an infinite cosmos and we happen to bump into each other?
CAMILLE KOCHANSKI: That is pretty incredible.
LISTER: And you realize: we have an awesome responsibility.
CAMILLE KOCHANSKI: We do?
LISTER: Sure we do: we have to rebuild the human race. As

quickly as possible. Shall we start now or d'you want to clean your teeth first?

CAMILLE KOCHANSKI: And they say romance is dead.

LISTER: Hey – the prospect of having to make love to a total stranger is just as galling to me, you know. But it's a vile and horrible obligation we're just going to have to endure. We've got to be totally professional about it. Totally clinical and unemotional. You just stay there and take it easy, and I'll go and slip into my Spiderman costume. It's funny, you really remind me of someone. You're so like her, it's untrue.

CAMILLE KOCHANSKI: Was she special?

LISTER: Special? She was the one, true love of my life, if you don't count lager milkshakes.

CAMILLE KOCHANSKI: So what happened?

LISTER: Oh, the usual. She took my heart and fed it through a car crusher. Came back about (*makes small shape*) this size with bits of an Austin Metro in it.

CAMILLE KOCHANSKI: She must have been insane.

RIMMER *comes in*.

RIMMER: Ah, Listy, I see you've met our ravishing guest. Have you seen Kryten?

HOLOGRAM CAMILLE: He's gone up to the penthouse quarters on A-deck.

RIMMER: Thanks muchly. (*Turns, turns back.*) Oh, listen, Camille, silly thought, really, but I thought perhaps when you're settled in and you're feeling up to it, perhaps we might pop up to the projection room and I can talk you through my photo collection of twentieth-century telegraph poles.

LISTER: Right, or, if you fancy a slightly more entertaining evening, you could let him take you outside and shoot you in the head.

RIMMER: As it happens, Listy, Camille's into telegraph poles every bit as much as I am. Especially the 1952 phase fours with the triple reinforced wire.

LISTER: Is this true?

CAMILLE KOCHANSKI: 'Course not.

RIMMER: You see? What did I tell you? She's also a big Reggie Wilson fan.

LISTER: You like Hammond organ music?

CAMILLE KOCHANSKI: Mindless pap.

RIMMER: Isn't it amazing? Telegraph poles, Reggie Wilson, it's uncanny how much we've got in common.

SHOT: HOLOGRAM CAMILLE.

LISTER: Are you OK, Rimmer?

RIMMER: Never better. Where was he? A-deck? Ciao for now.

RIMMER *goes.*

LISTER: What was all that about?

CAMILLE KOCHANSKI: All what?

LISTER: Come on: you were saying one thing and Rimmer was hearing another. How d'you do that?

CAMILLE KOCHANSKI: You'd have worked it out eventually, anyway. (*Pause*) I'm a pleasure GELF.

CUT TO:

14. Int. Corridor. Day

LISTER *turns out of lobby from medical unit and meets the* CAT.

CAT: What's going on, buddy? Eraserhead tells me she's a mechanoid, and Captain Sadness makes out she's a hologram.

LISTER: She's neither of those, and both of those. She's a GELF. A genetically engineered life-form. She's a pleasure GELF – created to be everyone's perfect companion. Everyone who looks at her perceives her differently. You see what you want to see: what you most desire.

CAT: Are you telling me if I go in that room, I'll see my perfect mate?

LISTER: Right. And she'll fall instantly in love with you.

CAT: Man, am I excited! What exquisite treasure of loveliness lies behind those doors?

LISTER: Knowing you, a six-foot Valkyrie warrior-maiden in scanty armour with a cleavage you can ski down.

CAT: Stop that talk – you're making me dribble. (*Straightens tie.*) Well, here goes.

CAT *goes towards medical unit.*

15. Int. Medical Unit. Day

The CAT *comes in and finds himself facing himself.*

CAT 2: Hi, buddy!

CAT: You're me!

CAT 2: Who else?

CAT: I'm the object of my own desire?

CAT 2: Can you think of anyone more deserving?

CAT: Well – when you put it like that – I guess you're right. Damn my vanity.

16. Int. Corridor. Day

LISTER *waiting. The* CAT *comes back out.*

LISTER: What did you see?

CAT: Oh, just some gorgeous chunk of loveliness. (*Sighs*) What a body. My legs are still shaking. Someone get me a brandy.

LISTER: Well, now we know what it is, we'd better tell the others.

17. Model shot. *Red Dwarf* in space

18. Int. Sleeping quarters. Day

KRYTEN, CAT, RIMMER, HOLLY *and* LISTER, *after the news has broken.*

RIMMER: Well. I should have guessed. It was all just a mighty bit too strange. I mean, actually meeting somebody who didn't want to vomit all over me in complete disgust and loathing.

KRYTEN: There's no need to take it so personally. It's the same for everyone – we've all been made to feel foolish, used, chewed up and spat out.

LISTER: Look, she didn't mean any harm. She can't control how we see her. She's like a mirror for our own obsessions.

KRYTEN: What did you see, Holly?

HOLLY: I didn't see anything. I don't think I've got any desires. Either that or my screen was foggy.

MECHANOID CAMILLE *appears at the door.*

MECHANOID CAMILLE: I guess I owe you all an apology.

SHOT: LISTER.

CAMILLE KOCHANSKI: I'm sorry, Dave.

SHOT: RIMMER.

HOLOGRAM CAMILLE: Sorry, Duke.

SHOT: CAT.

CAT 2: Sorry, buddy.
CAT: Heartbreaker!

SHOT: KRYTEN.

MECHANOID CAMILLE: I told you it wouldn't work, Kryten, if there were others. You're the one who's hurt the most – you're not used to these emotions.

KRYTEN: Why did you lie to me?

MECHANOID CAMILLE: Because I felt something really special for you – something I'd never felt before. I knew if you saw me as I really was, you'd be repelled.

KRYTEN: Try me.

MECHANOID CAMILLE: Turn away, and I'll change. I'll change to what I really am.

79

KRYTEN *turns away. The others don't.* CAMILLE *transforms into a large, amorphous green* BLOB, *completely unhuman-shaped, but with two eyes.*

BLOB: I'm ready.

KRYTEN *turns. His face betrays no emotion.*

BLOB: This is what I really look like.
KRYTEN: Oh.
BLOB: What d'you think?
KRYTEN: Well . . . I think you look very nice.
CAT: Nice? She looks like something that dropped out of the Sphinx's nose.
BLOB: He's right – I'm just a huge green blob.
KRYTEN: True, but as huge green blobs go, you're a really cute one.
BLOB: I don't believe you.
KRYTEN: OK, you're not ever going to get on the cover of *Vogue* – but, hey, neither am I. I think you're very sweet.
BLOB: You're lying.
KRYTEN: I can't lie – I'm a mechanoid.
BLOB: You really don't think I'm repulsive?
KRYTEN: Of course not. There are lots of humans not as attractive as you. Take Karl Malden. And he was a famous actor. You think this changes anything? Camille, I'd be honoured if you would agree to have dinner with me this evening.
BLOB: You mean that?
KRYTEN: Parrot's bar on G-deck. I'll meet you there at eight.
BLOB: Flats or heels?

CUT TO:

19. Model shot. *Red Dwarf* in space

20. Int. Sleeping quarters. Evening

CAT *and* RIMMER *are lounging around.* LISTER *comes in.*

CAT: I can't believe he's really going through with this.

RIMMER: Look, if Kryten wants to take out an amorphous green blob for a discreet tête-à-tentacle, I say good luck to him.

LISTER: Me too. I mean, we all react differently. When Steve McQueen met the Blob, he tried to kill it. It probably never crossed his mind to take it out to a restaurant.

CAT: I have an idea: they should go to a sushi bar – at least then the food won't look better than his date.

KRYTEN *comes in, in dinner-suit.*

KRYTEN: (*To* CAT) Sir, I respect your dress sense more than anything, and I'd really appreciate your opinion on this outfit.

CAT: Man, if I was going out with a large ball of green slime, that's how I'd dress.

KRYTEN: Thank you. That means a lot to me. Well. Don't wait up.

21. Int. Parrot's bar. Night

A sign reads: 'Parrot's', and stuffed parrots abound. Romantic music ('As Time Goes By' or something that sounds quite like it). KRYTEN *and* BLOB *having a romantic, candlelit dinner.* BLOB *with tentacle in soup bowl, slurping petitely.*

KRYTEN: Isn't this enchanting?

BLOB: Oh, Kryten – do you think we could make it, you and I?

KRYTEN: Of course – it's the old, old story: droid meets droid; droid becomes chameleon; droid loses chameleon; chameleon becomes blob; droid gets blob back again. It's the classic tale.

BLOB: A toast, my love.

If possible, they clink glasses.

BLOB: To us.

MIX TO:

MONTAGE:

22. Int. Parrot's. Night
Tables stacked, some with sheets. Romantic lighting. Smoke. KRYTEN *and* BLOB *dancing funkily.* MIX TO:

KRYTEN *and* BLOB *dancing romantically.* MIX TO:

23. Int. *Starbug* cockpit. Night
KRYTEN *and* BLOB *joyriding.* KRYTEN *regaling* BLOB *with anecdotes.* MIX TO:

24. Int. Ship's cinema. Night
KRYTEN *and* BLOB *watching* Casablanca. KRYTEN *tries to sneak his arm around the* BLOB. BLOB *sneaks tentacle around him.* KRYTEN *looks at the* BLOB, *obviously smitten.* HOLLY *appears on the cinema screen.*

KRYTEN: *Casablanca* — what a movie — I must have seen it a thousand times. Lister used to use it as part of my course. It's littered with examples of how lying can be noble.

BLOB: From now on, my darling, *Casablanca* will be our movie . . .

HOLLY: Hate to gooseberry, Kryten, but we've got a visitor down in the hangar. He wants to see Camille.

BLOB: I was going to tell you Kryten, truly I was. I have a clone mate.

KRYTEN: You have a husband?

BLOB: We're androgynous, but I suppose you could call him my 'husband'. Hector has a brilliant mind — he's been working on an antidote for our condition for years.

KRYTEN: Is Hector a blob, too?

BLOB: We're both blobs, Kryten. I left him a long time ago — I thought he'd given up looking.

KRYTEN: He really must think a lot of you.

BLOB: I guess.

BLOB *moves off.*

KRYTEN: Where are you going?

BLOB: I'm going to tell him I met someone else. I'm going to tell him I'm staying here with you.

MIX TO:

25. Int. *Red Dwarf* hangar. Night

Lots of swirly fog. We see a small section of a strange craft. LISTER, KRYTEN *and* BLOB *walk up.*

KRYTEN: Mr Lister, sir, would you be so kind as to take Camille's bag aboard?

LISTER: Certainly, Kryten, anything you say.

BLOB: Why my bag, Kryten?

KRYTEN: Because you're getting on that craft with Hector, where you belong.

BLOB: No, Kryten . . .

KRYTEN: Now, you've got to listen to me; do you have any idea what you've got to look forward to if you stay here?

BLOB: You're saying this only to make me go.

KRYTEN: We both know you belong to Hector – you're part of his work, the thing that keeps him going. If you're not on that craft when it leaves the hangar, you'll regret it, maybe not today, maybe not tomorrow, but soon, and for the rest of your life.

BLOB: What about us?

KRYTEN: We'll always have 'Parrot's'.

BLOB: Oh, Kryten . . .

KRYTEN: I'm no good at being noble, kid, but it's pretty obvious that the problems of two blobs and a droid don't amount to a hill of beans in this crazy cosmos.

HECTOR *the blob comes up.*

HECTOR: Are you ready, Camille?

BLOB: I'm ready. Goodbye, Kryten. And bless you.

The two BLOBS *go off. Music swells.* KRYTEN *watches them go.* LISTER *comes up.*

LISTER: You were lying, Kryten.

KRYTEN: Yes. It hurt to do it, but it was her best shot at happiness. It's the old, old story: droid meets droid; droid becomes chameleon; droid loses chameleon; chameleon turns into blob; droid gets blob back again; blob meets blob; blob goes off with blob, and droid loses blob, chameleon and droid. How many times have we seen that story?

LISTER: I suppose you're going to blame me for all of this.

KRYTEN: Yes, I am. Without your lessons, without your bananas and your movies and your aardvarks, none of this could have happened. You're a complete and total smeghead.

LISTER: Brutal, man. You just insulted me.

KRYTEN: Yes, I can lie, cheat and be offensive now.

They wander off.

LISTER: Kryten – this could be the start of a beautiful friendship.

Run credits

BACKWARDS

Opening roller

The following recap scrolls up the screen majestically, à la Star Wars, *gradually increasing in speed until it becomes totally unreadable:*

RED DWARF III
THE SAGA CONTINUUMS
THE STORY SO FAR . . .

Three million years in the future, Dave Lister, the last human being alive, discovers he is pregnant after a liaison with his female self in a parallel universe. His pregnancy concludes with the successful delivery of twin boys, Jim and Bexley. However, because they were conceived in another universe, with different physical laws, they suffer from highly accelerated growth rates, and are both eighteen years old within three days of being born. In order to save their lives, Lister returns them to the universe of their origin where they are reunited with their father (a woman) and are able to lead comparatively normal lives. Well, as normal as you can be if you've been born in a parallel universe and your father's a woman and your mother's a man and you're eighteen years old three days after your birth. Shortly afterwards, Kryten, the service mechanoid who'd left the ship after being rescued from his own crashed vessel, the Nova 5, is found in pieces after his space bike crash-lands into an asteroid. Lister rebuilds the 'noid, but is unable to recapture his former personality.

Meanwhile, Holly, the increasingly erratic *Red Dwarf* computer, performs a head sex change operation on himself. He bases his new face on Hilly, a female computer with whom he'd once fallen madly in love.

AND NOW THE SAGA CONTINUUMS ...
RED DWARF III
THE SAME GENERATION
— NEARLY

1. Int. Sleeping quarters. Night

Very very dark. LISTER *and the* CAT *are lying in the bunks, watching a mobile TV monitor opposite the bunks. We shoot over the monitor, so we don't see the TV.* LISTER *and the* CAT's *eyes never leave the TV screen. From the TV we hear the sounds of a cartoon. They fade under the dialogue:*

LISTER: (*Torpid — almost catatonic*) Cat?
CAT: (*Same*) Mm?
LISTER: You ever see the *Flintstones*?
CAT: Sure.

Long pause.

LISTER: Do you think Wilma's sexy?
CAT: Wilma Flintstone?
LISTER: Maybe we've been alone in Deep Space too long, but every time I see her on the show, that body drives me crazy. Is it me?
CAT: I think, in all probability, Wilma Flintstone is the most desirable woman who ever lived.
LISTER: That's good. I thought I was going strange.
CAT: She's incredible.
LISTER: What d'you think of Betty?
CAT: Betty Rubble? Well, I would go with Betty. (*Pause*) But I'd be thinking of Wilma.
LISTER: This is crazy. Why are we talking about going to bed with Wilma Flintstone?
CAT: You're right. We're nuts. This is an insane conversation.

Pause.

LISTER: She'll never leave Fred, and we know it.

2. Model shot. Cargo bay

ON ADO. There is a bench seat against one of the walls, which
KRYTEN *is sitting on. The massive-looking Starbug 1 is in the*
docking-bay.

3. PRE-VT: Int. Cargo bay. Day

A very nervous KRYTEN *is sitting on the bench seat. His right leg is*
jiggling maniacally, and he looks at his watch every three seconds. He
runs through a series of strange movements, which we don't quite under-
stand: reaching over his head, and activating imaginary levers, changing
an imaginary gearstick, looking in an imaginary driving-mirror, and so
on. RIMMER *strides up, holding a hologramatic clipboard and pencil.*
KRYTEN *leaps to his feet.*

RIMMER: Well, Krytie, today's the day.

KRYTEN: D'you really think I'm ready, Mr Rimmer, sir? Six
weeks . . . it's just not long enough . . .

RIMMER: (*Looks at watch*) Ten–thirty. (*Writes on clipboard*) Name?

KRYTEN: You know my name.

RIMMER: Look. If this comes off, it'll be a whole new lease of life
for both of us. We'll be independent – we'll be able to go
wherever we like whenever we like. But we have to do it by
the book.

KRYTEN: It's just . . . when you go into 'official' mode, my
anxiety chip goes into overdrive.

RIMMER: Name?

KRYTEN: K–K–K–K–K . . .

RIMMER: I'll just put 'Kryten'. Can you see that space vehicle?

KRYTEN: Where? Oh, right, that one. Yes, sir.

RIMMER: And can you read the registration for me, please?

KRYTEN *looks up at the huge sign on the side of the craft.*

KRYTEN: Uh, *Starbug 1*?

RIMMER *makes a discreet tick on his pad.*

RIMMER: Right. If you'd like to show me to your vehicle, please.

KRYTEN *waddles off towards the* Starbug.

4. Int. *Starbug* cockpit. Day

KRYTEN *is sitting in the driving-seat, putting on his safety-belt, with* RIMMER *beside him.*

RIMMER: Right. In your own time, would you like to start the space vehicle, proceed through the cargo bay doors, and off into outer space.

KRYTEN *presses a button and the engine starts up.* RIMMER *ticks his pad discreetly.* KRYTEN *presses another button and the windscreen wipers start up noisily. He grins, embarrassed, and turns them off.* RIMMER, *giving nothing away, makes another little mark on his pad.*

RIMMER: Once through the cargo bay doors, proceed directly to the nearest planet. Once there, I want you to bring the vehicle to a halt, and then carefully reverse into the planet's orbit, remembering, of course, at all times to pay due care and attention to any other space users. Right. In your own time.

KRYTEN *reaches down and pulls a lever.* RIMMER *looks up. There is a noise as the unseen roof above him slides back. Jets on his chair fire up, and* RIMMER *and his chair catapult out of shot.*

5. Model shot. Cargo bay

RIMMER *and chair eject through* Starbug's *roof.*

6. Int. *Starbug* cockpit. Day

KRYTEN, *slightly pained, looks back at* HOLLY, *who is expressionless. There is a pause.* RIMMER *climbs back into the bug, as if nothing has happened. He sits down, and looks at* KRYTEN, *who is staring fixedly out of the window, then makes another little mark on his pad.*

RIMMER: In your own time.
KRYTEN: I've failed, haven't I?
RIMMER: Just proceed.

KRYTEN: You're going to hold it against me, aren't you – that one mistake?

RIMMER: Please. (*Indicates* KRYTEN *should move off.*)

7. Model shot. Cargo bay

Starbug *is standing ready for take-off, jets smoking.*

KRYTEN: (*VO*) Anti-grav, check. Retro, check. Boosters, check.

Starbug *lifts up vertically and wobbles slightly. In front of them the cargo bay doors are open on to space.*

KRYTEN: (*VO*) And very gently ease forward.

A major jet on the back of the Starbug *bursts into life, and the ship rockets through the wall above the cargo bay doors.*

8. Int. *Starbug* cockpit. Day

The engines are whining slightly, as an inexperienced hand struggles to master the vehicle. There is a horrible gear change. KRYTEN *turns to* RIMMER.

KRYTEN: I think there's something wrong with the gear box. The thing is – I learnt to drive in *Starbug 2*, I'm not really used to the controls in *Starbug 1*.

RIMMER: They're exactly the same.

KRYTEN: Yes. That's the problem.

9. Model shot

Starbug *wobbling through space.*

10. Int. *Starbug* cockpit. Day

KRYTEN *is concentrating fiercely and stiffly on driving badly.*

RIMMER: Next, I'd like you to transfer to autopilot, while we conduct the recognition tests.

KRYTEN *crunches a gear change.*

KRYTEN: Engage autopilot.
HOLLY: Autopilot engaged. Well, I say 'autopilot', but it's not really 'autopilot' is it? It's me, it's muggins here who has to do it.

'Autopilot' comes up on the monitors. KRYTEN *takes the large book from beside* RIMMER, *and opens it.* RIMMER *points to a sign.*

RIMMER: What's that one?
KRYTEN: 'Heavy traffic – keep to your assigned space lane.'
RIMMER: This?

We see RIMMER *is pointing at a sign which is a silhouette of a rampant woman waving a bra.*

KRYTEN: 'Danger – space mirages ahead.'
RIMMER: And this?
KRYTEN: If you'll pardon my saying – I've got a photographic memory, so I'm bound to get all these right.
RIMMER: This?
KRYTEN: 'Give priority to Halley's comet.' That's rather silly – as if you wouldn't.
RIMMER: Stopping distances. You are travelling half the speed of light – what's the stopping distance?
KRYTEN: Four years, three months.
RIMMER: And the thinking time?
KRYTEN: A fortnight.

RIMMER *points at the book again.*

RIMMER: Space phenomena. What's that?
KRYTEN: A pulsar.
RIMMER: And that?
KRYTEN: A binary star.
RIMMER: This one?

In the front viewscreen we see a brightly coloured, weird-looking spirally thing in space, swirling towards them.

HOLLY: A time-hole!

RIMMER: Don't help him!

KRYTEN: It's a time-hole!

RIMMER raises his eyebrows.

RIMMER: No, it isn't. It's nothing like a time-hole.

HOLLY: It's a time-hole!

KRYTEN: It is! It's a time-hole.

RIMMER: It's nothing like a time-hole. A time-hole is a phenom-
enon rarely seen in space, which legend would have us believe
transports us into another part of space and time. Whereas this
is quite clearly a blue giant about to go super-nova. (*Looks out
of the windscreen*) *That* is a time-hole! . . . Right. Next one.
What's this?

Slowly it dawns on RIMMER. He looks up.

RIMMER: (*Quietly*) Oh, smeg.

11. FX shot
Starbug's *POV*: *2001ish type trip through the time-hole.*

12. Model shot
Starbug, *burning through cloudy stratosphere.*

13. OB. Ext. Forest near lake. Day
*Birds twittering, etc. Suddenly we hear Starbug in a death dive.
SHOT: cute animal (squirrel or deer or something) suddenly hears
something and looks up. Still on the animal, we hear a huge crash,
followed by a boiling hiss.*

14. OB. Ext. Lakeside. Day
Frothing and bubbling. Some Starbug wreckage bobs to the surface.

15. Int. *Starbug* cockpit. Underwater.

Starbug is at the bottom of the lake, tilted forward radically, lit very darkly. Water on the viewscreens, although we can't see very much. KRYTEN *looks at* RIMMER. RIMMER *looks at* KRYTEN. *They look at one another for a long time.*

KRYTEN: I suppose you're going to fail me for this.

16. OB. Ext. Lakeside. Day

KRYTEN *is mooring a silver space dinghy to the lakeside.*

KRYTEN: What is this place?
RIMMER: Holly? Is it possible? Could this be Earth?

HOLLY *appears on* KRYTEN*'s wrist monitor.*

HOLLY: It certainly seems that way – constellations match, gravity exactly one G. . . .
RIMMER: What's the time period?
HOLLY: Well, it's difficult to pin it down exactly, but according to all the available data, I would estimate it's probably round about lunchtime. Maybe half-one.
RIMMER: What period in history, dingleberry breath?
HOLLY: Oh, I see . . .
RIMMER: I mean, can we expect to see Ghengis Khan and his barbarian buddies sweeping over the hill? Or perhaps a herd of flesh-eating dinosaurs, feeding off the bones of Doug McClure? What is the year?
HOLLY: Well, I'd need some more data before I can give you a precise answer.
RIMMER: Like?
HOLLY: Well, this year's calendar'd be handy.

17. OB. Ext. Forest. Day

RIMMER *leads the way.* KRYTEN *is looking at a tree.*

KRYTEN: I've never been to Earth before. I've only seen it on photographs. It's exactly like I always imagined, only much shorter.

18. OB. Ext. Roadside. Day

RIMMER and KRYTEN *are standing before a roadsign:* 'NODNOL 891 SELIM'

RIMMER: 'Nodnol 891 selim?' Nodnol? Where's Nodnol?
KRYTEN: It's 'London'. 'London 198 miles'. It's backwards.
RIMMER: Shhhh. A truck.

They stand by the side of the road, holding thumbs out, hopefully. The sound of the truck grows louder. As they stand in the foreground of the picture, a truck appears over the brow of a hill, behind them. The truck is going backwards. It reverses past them, and stops.

RIMMER: There's a perfectly rational explanation for this.

The DRIVER *leans out of the window and hikes his thumb, to indicate they should jump in the back of the truck.*

DRIVER: (*Backwards*) Hop in! I'm going into town, if you're looking for a lift.
RIMMER: Then again, perhaps not.

19. OB. City centre. Day
All the traffic going backwards, including the truck with RIMMER *and* KRYTEN *in it.*

20. OB. Ext. Busy shopping street. Day
Everybody walking backwards, except for KRYTEN *and* RIMMER, *who are walking forwards.*

RIMMER: Holly, what the smeg is going on?
KRYTEN: Everything's going backwards.
HOLLY: It's perfectly consistent with current theory. Everything starts with the Big Bang, and the Universe starts expanding.

Eventually, when it's expanded as far as it can, there's the Big Crunch and everything starts contracting. Perfectly possible that time starts running in the opposite direction, too.

RIMMER: So is this Earth?

HOLLY: Oh, it's Earth, all right. Only, an Earth where time is running backwards.

21. Int. Café. Day

Small café counter and two tables are visible. All writing, naturally, is backwards. RIMMER *is sitting alone at a table, covering his 'H', and trying not to stare at the* GIRL *at the table beside him. A* WAITRESS *walks up to the* GIRL*, backwards, puts down an empty plate and empty glass coffee cup.*

WAITRESS: (*Backwards*) Was everything OK?

GIRL: (*Backwards*) Yes, thank you. It was delicious.

As RIMMER *watches out of the side of his eyes, the* GIRL *starts to fill up the glass cup with coffee from her mouth, and in three 'un-bites' reconstitutes a chocolate éclair. When the glass cup is finally full, the* GIRL *puts her teaspoon in it, stirs it round, then lifts two spoons of clean granulated sugar from the coffee and dumps them into the sugar bowl. She glances across at* RIMMER*, staring at her.*

GIRL: (*Backwards*) The service here is terrible.

RIMMER: (*Smiles charmingly*) Flobadob, blib blob bleeb.

KRYTEN *comes in, holding a newspaper, wearing a Ronald Reagan mask and a black Darth Vader cloak. He sits next to* RIMMER.

RIMMER: What are you doing?

KRYTEN: You said 'Look inconspicuous'.

RIMMER: Get them off!

KRYTEN: But if people see my face, what are they going to think?

RIMMER: Just tell them you had an accident. Tell them you took your car to the crushers, and forgot to get out.

The WAITRESS *comes up, empties debris from a box and smears the table with a filthy cloth.*

KRYTEN: I got a newspaper.

RIMMER *leans over his shoulder.*

RIMMER: What year is it? Thirty-nine ninety-one?!

KRYTEN: It's 1993. It's backwards. I'll switch to reverse mode: (*Reads*) 'THREE BROUGHT TO LIFE IN BANK RAID – A masked man with a sawn-off shotgun sucked bullets out of two cashiers and a security guard in a South London bank tomorrow. The masked raider then forced terrified staff to accept £10,000 in unmarked notes, which he then demanded were placed in the bank's vaults. The man, Michael Ellis, completed a fifteen-year prison sentence for the crime two years ago.'

RIMMER: (*Points at paper*) What does that say?

KRYTEN: It's an advert: 'Roll-off deodorant – keeps you wet and smelly for up to 24 hours.' What are we going to do? This place is totally crazy.

RIMMER: There's nothing we can do until the others find us. We'll have to get a job. But what kind of jobs are there in a backwards reality for a dead hologram and an android with a head shaped like a novelty condom?

KRYTEN: Here's the jobs page. What about this: 'Wanted: Managing Director, ICI. Excellent demotion prospects. Right candidate could go straight to the bottom'.

RIMMER: Something a bit more low key.

KRYTEN: (*Reads*) 'Busy London restaurant requires dish-dirtier'.

RIMMER: Anything else?

KRYTEN: Oh, this looks quite interesting. 'Theatrical Agent requires novelty acts'.

RIMMER: What do we do that's a novelty?

KRYTEN: In this world – everything.

22. Model shot. *Red Dwarf* in space

Starbug 2 *leaving the ship.*

23. Int. *Starbug* cockpit. Night

LISTER *is at the controls. The* CAT *is in the passenger seat.*

CAT: Three weeks we've been doing this.

LISTER: Well, we'll do it till we find them.

CAT: We ain't gonna find 'em – (*Sadly*) They're gone, buddy. But, look on the bright side: (*brightly*) they're gone, buddy!

LISTER: Don't you care about anybody but yourself?

CAT: Hell, no. I don't even care about you. The way I see it, if Goalpost Head and Freak Face want to get themselves lost, that's their bag. I don't see why it should cut into my preening time. You realize, with all this rescue stuff, I haven't permed my leg hairs in a week! I'm a wreck, buddy.

LISTER: You perm your leg hairs?

CAT: Only as an aid to the natural curl.

LISTER: (*Suddenly serious*) Fasten your belt.

CAT: Hey, I do not need fashion tips from you.

LISTER: Your safety belt. Look!

We see the time-hole looming up.

CAT: Is that what I think it is?

LISTER: What d'you think it is?

CAT: An orange whirly thing in space.

LISTER: It's a time-hole. That's where they are. And we're going in.

CAT: Are you crazy? We can't go in there.

LISTER: Why not?

CAT: Orange? With this suit?

24. FX shot: Journey through time-hole

25. OB. Ext. Field. Day

Starbug 2 *flying across.*

26. Int. *Starbug 2* cockpit. Day

CAT: Where are we?

LISTER: This is incredible: according to the NaviComp, this is Earth! I'm taking her down. Engage cloak.

Presses button marked 'Cloak'.

27. OB. Ext. Field. Day

Starbug 2 *descending. Suddenly, with an appropriate SFX, it becomes invisible. Wind-machine blasts at the ground, as the invisible craft lands. Engine sounds stop. We hear an airlock being opened, and* LISTER *emerges, followed by the* CAT, *about eight feet in the air, and they start walking down invisible steps to the ground.*

CAT: What d'you do that for?

LISTER: Don't want to freak the natives.

They get down to the ground.

LISTER: (*Winces*) Ah! My ribs.

CAT: What's the matter?

LISTER: Dunno. My ribs feel like they're cracked . . . and my back. Ah! Is my eye bruised?

CAT: A little.

LISTER *produces a tracking device and starts operating it.*

CAT: What's that?

LISTER: It's a homing device. It'll find their flight recorder. (*Gets a bearing. Nods.*) Yonder.

They set off.

LISTER: I'm home.

28. OB. Ext. Lakeside. Day

CAT *standing by the lake.* LISTER*'s head breaks the surface, and he starts swimming to the shore.*

SHOT: CAT.

CAT: Find anything?
LISTER: The '*bug*'s there, but they're not.

SHOT: LISTER *wades out of the lake and on to the bank (reversed).*

SHOT: CAT

CAT: You're dry!
LISTER: Yeah. That's weird.
CAT: Let's take a look around. Maybe they left a clue.
LISTER: That's really weird.

29. OB. Ext. Forest. Day

CAT *and* LISTER, *wandering along. There are posters nailed to some of the trees.* LISTER *rips one down.*

LISTER: What's this?

There is a photo of RIMMER *and* KRYTEN *in showbizzy outfits, over which is printed:* 'SREHTORB ESREVER LANOITASNES EHT' *and, underneath, a backwards address.*

LISTER: They must have pinned these up, to tell us where they'll be.
CAT: What's it say?
LISTER: I dunno. It's in some weird foreign language. 'Srehtorb'? Sounds Polish or Bulgarian or something.
CAT: You speak Bulgarian?
LISTER: Me? I can barely speak English.

30. OB. Ext. Roadside. Day

CAT *and* LISTER, *walking down the road, come up to the roadsign.*

LISTER: 'Nodnol'. Wait a minute . . . wait a minute . . . 'Nodnol' is in Bulgaria.

CAT: Are you sure?

LISTER: Absolutely. Geography was my best subject at school. Nodnol. Bulgaria. Rich in animal produce and mineral wealth. Just south of Bosnia.

CAT: What's 'selim'?

LISTER: Selim. Obviously it's Bulgarian for 'kilometres'.

CAT: You're so smart. I'm glad I came with you.

LISTER: Let's find some transport. (*Winces*) Ah! My smegging ribs.

31. OB. Ext. Different bit of roadside. Day

A COUPLE *are snoozing on some grass. Beside them are a tandem and a picnic hamper.* LISTER *and* CAT *sneak up, pick up the bike, and run down the road with it, as quietly as possible. When they're about thirty yards away from the* COUPLE:

LISTER: OK.

They start to mount the bike. There is a cry behind them. The COUPLE *are standing in the road.*

BIKE MAN: (*Swears at them backwards*)
SUBTITLE: You scoundrels! Return my bike immediately!
LISTER: OK, come on – get on – go go go!

CAT, *on the back of the tandem, swivels round in his saddle.*

CAT: Bye, suckers. You lost your bike.
LISTER: Start pedalling! Start pedalling!

They both start pedalling. The tandem shoots off backwards.

CAT: What the hell's happening? Get this thing in forward gear!
LISTER: It *is* in forward gear!

They pedal right up to the baffled COUPLE, *and past them.*

32. OB. Ext. Another part of the roadside. Day

There is a van parked in a lay-by. LISTER *and the* CAT *come into shot backwards on the tandem.*

CAT: Stop! Stop!

They get off the bike.

CAT: No more, man. I'm not moving another yard on this thing. I'm getting a parting in the back of my head!

LISTER *kicks the bike.*

LISTER: Goddam cheap Bulgarian bikes! You probably have to queue up for a year to get this piece of crap. You probably have to be a government official to get one that goes forwards!

Kicks it again. The VAN DRIVER *comes out of the woods and heads for his vehicle.*

LISTER: Hello? Excuse me?
VAN DRIVER: (*Backwards*) Pardon?
LISTER: We don't speak any Bulgarian. Do you speak English?
VAN DRIVER: (*Speaks backwards*)
SUBTITLE: Sorry, I'm English. Are you Bulgarians?
LISTER: Uh, we're looking for our friends-ski . . .

LISTER *holds up the poster.*

CAT: Our buddy-ski. Our palski.
LISTER: There's an address-ski, here-ski. (*Points to poster*) Can you drop us off-ski?
VAN DRIVER: (*Speaks backwards*)
SUBTITLE: Yes, I know this pub. Sure. Hop in the back.

He points to the back of the van.

LISTER: OK, we're on.
CAT: Thankski veryski muchski, budski.

CAT *and* LISTER *climb in the back of the van and close the door.*

CAT: (*VO*) Hey hey hey! We're moving in the right direction, now.

The van starts up and reverses off.

33. Film: stock. City at night
Deserted. Quiet.

34. Int. Stairwell to pub. Night
LISTER *and* CAT *come down the stairs. There is a billboard with a photo, over which is splashed:* 'ETINOT EVIL'.

LISTER: This is the place.
CAT: Hey, your eye – it's getting worse.
LISTER: Not as bad as my back. Feels like it's been cut to ribbons.
CAT: Moan, moan, moan, moan, moan.

35. Int. Pub. Night
Very dimly lit, except for a couple of spots on the small, makeshift stage. An MC *is at the MIC.*

MC: (*Speaks backwards*)
SUBTITLE: Ladies and gentlemen, I want you to take your hands apart and give a big warm goodbye to the Sensational Reverse Brothers!

Silly magician music, KRYTEN *and* RIMMER *come on stage, dressed in ludicrous low-life showbiz gear.* KRYTEN *is carrying a little magician's fold-up table with various props on it. We see* LISTER *and the* CAT *standing at the back. Everyone is watching the stage.*

RIMMER: Hello, and welcome to the show.

Big backwards laugh.

LISTER: (*To* CAT) Hello and welcome to the show? That's a joke??

RIMMER: For our first trick, my partner will attempt to eat a boiled egg! (*Long pause.*) Forwards!

AUDIENCE *look at one another in amazement.* KRYTEN *cuts the top off the boiled egg. Huge laugh. He starts eating it. Hysterics.*

CAT: This is entertainment to these people? It's pathetic.

LISTER: They're Bulgarians. They have very simple tastes.

KRYTEN *tosses the empty shell to someone in the crowd, who examines it, baffled. Huge, backwards applause, laughing backwards. They look like barking seals.*

CAT: I have it. It's a Moron Convention. Look at them, they can barely clap. Check the cloakroom. If there are twenty jackets, all white, with arms that tie behind the neck, you know I'm right.

RIMMER: And what better way to round off a meal, than by drinking a glass of water? Kryten?

LISTER: Woha! Stick around. They're building up to a big climax.

CAT: Just how is he gonna do this one? Mirrors?

KRYTEN *drinks the water, to gasps from the audience. More applause.* LISTER *and* CAT *exchange looks.*

RIMMER: We are the Sensational Reverse Brothers, Ladies and Gentlemen. We shall see you last night!

RIMMER *and* KRYTEN *dance off the stage to their theme tune. Once the lights are up, we see it's a dog-rough pub. There is evidence of a recent bar-brawl – smashed chairs, tables on end. A large window is smashed. Through it we see a brick wall. One* MAN *is lying in a bloody stupor, amid some debris, as* CAT *and* LISTER *walk up to the bar.*

LISTER: Nice pub. If you've still got both your ears, you're not a regular. Come on. Let's grab a pint and go backstage.

A man, the MANAGER, *is sitting on a barstool, with half a pint of beer in front of him. He is reading a backwards newspaper.*

LISTER: (*Calls*) Hello?

A WOMAN *behind the bar walks up to them backwards, and smiles.*

LISTER: Hi. Can I have two pints of bitter, please?

The WOMAN *looks at him oddly.*

LISTER: Bitter? Two pints?
CAT: She doesn't understand you, bud. You're wasting your time.

The WOMAN *looks round at the* MANAGER *drinking at the bar.*

LISTER: What's that you're drinking? (*Points at the manager's drink*) Drinkee. Beerski.
MANAGER: Erskib.
LISTER: Erskib. Right. Two pints of erskib.
WOMAN: Erskib?

LISTER *holds up two fingers.*

LISTER: See? Was that a big deal? Was that hard?
WOMAN: Erskib . . .

She puts a used empty pint pot on the bar.

WOMAN: Erskib . . .

She puts down a second empty pot and hands LISTER *some money. He looks at the empty beer glasses, and then at the money in his hand. They glance across at the* MANAGER, *who raises the half-full pint pot to his lips, and fills it up to the top. The* WOMAN *goes, backwards, to the* MANAGER, *picks up his now-full pint.*

MANAGER: (*Speaks backwards*)
SUBTITLE: Same again.

She takes his full pint, puts it under the pump and sucks all the beer out. REACTION SHOT: CAT *and* LISTER, *watching. She hands back the empty glass. He nods a thank you and starts to fill it up again.*

LISTER: This isn't Bulgaria.

Grabs bar menu.

LISTER: Look at the menu. 'UNEM'. It's English, but backwards. Everything's backwards.
CAT: Everything's backwards? Right!

They look at their empty glasses.

LISTER: Well, as they say: when in Rome, do as the snamor do.

LISTER *and the* CAT *pick up their glasses and clank them together.*

LISTER: Well. Up the hatch.
CAT: Booties down.

They fill their pint pots.

36. Int. Dressing-room. Night
*Small, grotty-looking dressing-room. The door is ajar. Two mirrors
with bare lightbulbs around them.* RIMMER *and* KRYTEN *on chairs,
with their backs to the mirrors,* CAT *and* LISTER *on two other
chairs.*

LISTER: What do you mean, you don't want to leave?
RIMMER: We're happy here.
KRYTEN: We've found a niche.
RIMMER: The Sensational Reverse Brothers. We've only been
here three weeks, and we're a smash.
CAT: But everything's backwards!
KRYTEN: We've got used to it.
RIMMER: He's right. Once you get over the initial shocks, things
actually make a lot more sense this way round! There's no
death here. You start off dead. You have a funeral, then you
come to life! As each year passes, you get younger and younger until you become a new-born baby. Then you go back
inside your mother, who goes back inside her mother, and so
on, until we all become one glorious whole.
LISTER: Rimmer, you already *are* one glorious hole. You've totally flipped, man.

KRYTEN: We want to stay.

LISTER: We can't stay. Look: I'm twenty-five now – in ten years' time, I'll be fifteen. I'll have to go through puberty again. Backwards.

CAT: Imagine that. Your pubic hairs will retract into your body. Your gajumbas will suddenly rise, and next thing you know you're singing soprano in the school choir.

LISTER: And worse – in twenty-five years, I'll be a little sperm, swimming around in someone's testicles. Pardon me, but that's just not how I saw my future.

RIMMER: I'm telling you, things are better this way. It's our universe that's the wrong way round.

KRYTEN: Take war. War is a wonderful thing here. In less than fifty years, the Second World War will start, backwards.

CAT: And that's a good thing?

KRYTEN: Millions of people will come to life. Hitler will retreat across Europe . . . liberate France and Poland, disband the Third Reich and bog off back to Austria.

RIMMER: We're smash hits here. We'd be crazy to leave.

LISTER: Rimmer, we don't belong here. This is a crazy place.

RIMMER: Crazy? Death, disease, war, famine – there's none of that here.

KRYTEN: There's no crime. The first night we were here, a mugger jumped us and forced fifty pounds into my wallet at knife-point.

LISTER: Yeah, but look at the flip side of the coin – someone like . . . say . . . St Francis of Assisi. In this universe, he's a petty-minded little sadist who goes around maiming small animals. Or Santa Claus – what a bastard!

RIMMER: Eh?

LISTER: Well, he's just a big fat git who sneaks down chimneys and steals all the kids' favourite toys.

Suddenly the MANAGER *storms in backwards.*

MANAGER: (*A tirade of backwards invective we don't understand.*)

KRYTEN: What fight? We didn't start any fight.

RIMMER: What's he saying?

MANAGER: (*More backwards invective.*)

MANAGER *then walks backwards out of the door. Pause. He knocks on the door three times.*

KRYTEN: He's fired us. Something about a fight.

LISTER: But you've been with us all night.

KRYTEN: He says we'll never work the pub circuit again. Says we're trouble makers.

RIMMER: What's he talking about?

37. PRE-VT. Int. Pub. Night

LISTER *and the* CAT *are sitting at a table, while* KRYTEN *and* RIMMER *argue, out of earshot, with the* MANAGER. *There is an empty pot already there, and a plate with a small piece of pie crust on the table.*

CAT: What's all that about?

LISTER: Who knows? Rimmer in a fight? That's a laugh for a start.

CAT: So, what's the plan?

LISTER: I dunno. See what happens, and if they don't change their minds, head back without 'em, I suppose. (*Winces*) My back – it feels like it's cut to ribbons.

LISTER *absently picks up the pie crust, puts the crust to his mouth, and regurgitates a whole wedge-shaped section of pork pie. The* CAT *picks up the piece and regurgitates another section.* LISTER *picks up the now half-complete pie and regurgitates another quarter. The* CAT *picks it up and completes the pie. The* CAT *then reaches into his mouth, and pulls out a slice of cucumber, which he puts on the plate by the pie.* LISTER *does the same with a slice of tomato. Then they both produce a lettuce leaf each, to complete the garnish.*

CAT: We have got to get out of here. This universe is just too disgusting.

A MAN *comes in, backwards from the loo, and goes up to their table. He looks down at the pie, wide-eyed in disbelief, and then accusingly at them.*

MAN 2: (*Backwards invective.*)

CAT: What's the matter with him?

MAN 2: (*Backwards invective.*)

LISTER: I think he's a bit teed-off because you've just uneaten his pie.

RIMMER *and* KRYTEN *have wandered over.*

RIMMER: Unbelievable! We didn't start a fight.

LISTER: Oh sorry, man, uh . . . we . . .

MAN 2 *punches* LISTER *in the face.* LISTER *clutches his eye.*

CAT: Are you all right?

LISTER: My black eye. It's gone! He sucked it off my face with his fist.

The PIE MAN *delivers a hefty body punch to* LISTER*'s ribs.*

LISTER: Now he's un-cracked my ribs.

RIMMER: Look, we don't want any trouble, we don't want any trouble – I'm not with them.

KRYTEN: No – you don't understand – all this mess, all this debris – this is from the fight we got fired for! This is a fight we're about to have!

RIMMER: About to have? I don't want to be involved in a bar room brawl!

LISTER: It's not a bar room brawl – it's a bar room tidy! (*Shouts gleefully*) Un-rumble!

The backwards fight commences: the GUY *in the stupor staggers up,* KRYTEN *passes the* CAT *a broken chair, the* CAT *then un-smashes it over the* GUY*'s head, and passes it back to* KRYTEN*, who puts it neatly under the table.* ANOTHER MAN *picks up a broken bottle, brings it up against the bar, and puts the now-whole bottle on the bar.* LISTER *starts to go out of the door.*

RIMMER: (*Hiding under a table*) Where are you going, you coward?

LISTER: I've just worked out what happens to my back.

He goes out of the door. A MAN *rushes to the middle of the pub.* LISTER *flies in through the window, backwards. The window reconstitutes itself behind him. The* MAN *catches* LISTER, *and grins so we see his middle tooth is missing.*

LISTER: Thanks, pal. Have your tooth back.

LISTER *punches him in the mouth. The* MAN *grins, and we see his tooth is back in place. Finally, the pub gets completely tidied, and everyone sits down, and starts drinking quietly again.* RIMMER *gets up from the table he's been cowering under and dusts himself off.*

RIMMER: Good one, gentlemen. Thanks for your support.

They walk out, backwards. A pause. The CAT *comes back in.*

CAT: I've forgotten something.

He goes up to the bar, picks up the charity box, empties the money into his hand. The WOMAN *grins a thanks at him.*

CAT: What the hell? It's a good cause.

38. OB. Ext. Country road. Day

Taxi reverses down the road and stops. The CREW *get out.* LISTER *leans in the driver's window. The* DRIVER *gives him fifteen pounds.* LISTER *walks off.*

TAXI DRIVER: (*Shouts 'Oi' backwards.*)

LISTER *goes back.* TAXI DRIVER *gives him a 50p tip. Lister looks at it disdainfully.*

LISTER: Tight git.

39. OB. Ext. Field. Day

They climb the invisible steps to Starbug 2. KRYTEN *is just vanishing inside.* RIMMER *pauses on the stairs,* LISTER *behind him.* RIMMER *surveys the landscape.*

RIMMER: It could have worked, you know. It really could.

LISTER *shakes his head.*

RIMMER: Where's the Cat?
LISTER: He won't be long.

RIMMER *looks quizzical.*

LISTER: He's in the bushes.

RIMMER *understands. They stand there, thinking about it.*

LISTER: We've got to stop him.

But as they turn, the CAT *emerges from the bushes with an expression of horror on his face. He walks stiffly towards them. He climbs the steps — the face of a man who's just been to hell and back. He passes them. Back to them and the camera:*

CAT: Don't ask.

Run credits

KRYTEN

1. Model shot

Desolate asteroid surface. A crashed space ship: Nova 5. *We zoom in to one of the portholes, and hear dialogue from a TV soap opera.*

WOMAN: (*VO*) Sit down, Brook: there's something I want to tell you.

MAN: (*VO*) What is it, Kelly?

2. Int. Service deck, *Nova 5.* Day

The whole set is on a slant. It's the equivalent of the servants' quarters: basically, a fairly shabby, used-looking kitchen. We pan round to the back of a chair, in which someone, unseen, is watching the soap. A white gloved hand reaches into a box on a table and takes out a chocolate.

WOMAN: (*VO*) That night I said I was staying at Simone's . . .

MAN: (*VO*) Yes?

WOMAN: (*VO*) I wasn't.

We see the screen for the first time: it's an android soap opera. The 'man' and the 'woman' are TWO IDENTICAL-LOOKING METALLIC ANDROIDS *(called 'mechanoids').*

MECHANOID MAN: (*VO*) What?

MECHANOID WOMAN: I wasn't with Simone that evening, Brook. I spent the night with Gary.

MECHANOID MAN: Your ex-husband Gary? My business rival? What are you telling me, Kelly?

MECHANOID WOMAN: I'm saying . . . Brook Junior . . .
MECHANOID MAN: What about Brook Junior?
MECHANOID WOMAN: He isn't your android.

Freeze. Soap titles, and sig. tune:

SIG: 'Androids . . .
Everybody needs good androids.
Androids . . .
Should be good and should be true.
Androids . . .
Tho' we're only made of metal
Androids have feelings . . .'

Halfway through the music, we see the chair's occupant for the first time. He's a MECHANOID, *too. He is agog at this tremendous kicker in the plotline, a chocolate poised in front of his mouth. A microwave timing pinger goes off, and the mechanoid (*KRYTEN*) picks up the phone.*

KRYTEN: (*Into phone*) Lunch is ready, Miss Anne. Could you tell everybody else.
SIG: 'Androids have feelings . . .
   Androids have feelings, too . . .'

3. Int. Sleeping quarters. Day

LISTER *is cleaning his space bike: a jet-powered motorbike without wheels.* RIMMER *is pacing about, learning a language course from the vid screen:*

ESPERANTO TEACHER: *Mi esperas ke kiam vi venos la vetero estos milda.*

The TEACHER *pauses for the reply.*

RIMMER: Errm . . . Uhhh . . . Uhmmmm . . . wait a minute . . . I know this . . . Ooh . . . hang on . . . don't tell me . . . Urrrh . . .
LISTER: (*Without looking up*) I hope when you come, the weather will be clement.

ESPERANTO TEACHER: I hope when you come, the weather will be clement.

RIMMER: (*To* LISTER) Don't tell me – I would have got that.

ESPERANTO TEACHER: *Bonvolu direkti min al kvinstela hotelo?*

RIMMER: Oooh, yes . . . I remember this from last time . . . arhhhh . . .

LISTER: Please could you direct me to a five-star hotel?

RIMMER: Wrong, actually. Totally, completely and utterly wrong.

ESPERANTO TEACHER: Please could you direct me to a five-star hotel?

RIMMER: Lister, will you please shut up?

LISTER: I'm only helping you.

RIMMER: Well, I don't need any help.

ESPERANTO TEACHER: *La mango estis bonega! Plej korajn gratuloju al la kuiristo?*

RIMMER: (*Snaps finger*) I should like to purchase the inflatable orange beachball and that small bucket and spade.

ESPERANTO TEACHER: The meal was splendid! My heartiest congratulations to the chef.

RIMMER: Is it? Pause.

The vid pauses.

LISTER: Rimmer, you've been studying Esperanto now for eight years. How come you're so hopeless?

RIMMER: Oh, speaks. And how many books have you read in your entire life? The same number as Champion the Wonder Horse. Zero.

LISTER: I've read books.

RIMMER: We're not talking about books where the main character is a dog called 'Ben'. Not those kinds of books, with five cardboard pages, three words a page and a guarantee on the back which says: 'This book is waterproof and chewable'.

LISTER: I went to art college.

RIMMER: You!?

LISTER: Yeah.

RIMMER: How did *you* get into art college?

LISTER: Usual way. Usual normal way you get into art college. Failed all my exams, applied and they snapped me up.

RIMMER: You didn't get a degree, did you?

LISTER: No. Dropped out. I wasn't there long.

RIMMER: How long?

LISTER: Ninety-seven minutes. I thought it'd be a good skive, but I took one look at the timetable and checked out. It was ridiculous. I had lectures first thing in the afternoon. Half-past twelve every day. Who's together by then? You can still taste the toothpaste.

RIMMER: Well, unlike you, I have ambitions. I'm not content to sit around all day, polishing my space bike so I can go joy-riding through some asteroid belt. Because I'm not a git. And one of my ambitions is to learn a second language. Kindly let me get on with it. Play!

ESPERANTO TEACHER: *La menuo aspktas bonege. Mi provas la kokidajon.*

RIMMER: Ah, now. This one I do know.

HOLLY *replaces the woman on the screen.*

HOLLY: The menu looks excellent. I'll try the chicken.

RIMMER: Holly, as the Esperantinos would say: (*as if delivering an insult*) 'Bonvolu alsendi las pordistion – lausajne estas rano en mia bideo.'

RIMMER *flicks his thumb against his teeth in Holly's direction.*

RIMMER: And I think we all know what that means.

HOLLY: Yeah. It means: 'Could you send up the hall porter, there appears to be a frog in my bidet.'

RIMMER: Does it? Well what's that one about 'Your father was a baboon's rump and your mother spent most of her life up against a wall with sailors'?

HOLLY: I'm not telling you.

RIMMER: It's because you're bored, isn't it? That's why you're both annoying me.

HOLLY: I'm not bored. I've had a very busy morning. I devised a system to totally revolutionize music.

LISTER: Get outta town!

HOLLY: Yeah. I've decimalized it. Instead of the octave, it's the decative. I've invented two new notes: H and J.

LISTER: You can't just invent new notes.

HOLLY: Well, I have. Now it goes: doh, ray, mi, fah, soh, lah, woh, boh, ti, doh. Doh, ti, boh, woh, lah, soh, fah, mi, ray, doh.

RIMMER: What are you drivelling about?

HOLLY: Hol Rock. It'll be a whole new sound. All the instruments will be extra big, to incorporate my two new notes. Triangles with four sides, piano keyboards the length of zebra crossings. 'Course, women will be banned from playing the cello.

LISTER: Holly?

HOLLY: Yeah?

LISTER: Shut up.

HOLLY: Oh, I forgot. I haven't told you the news.

RIMMER: What news?

HOLLY: A signal. We're getting a signal. It's probably nothing, but I thought I'd mention it.

RIMMER: Aliens!

LISTER: Aliens? Your explanation for anything slightly odd is 'Aliens'. You lose your keys, it's 'Aliens'. A picture falls off the wall, it's 'Aliens'. That time we used up a whole bog roll in a day, you thought it was Aliens.

RIMMER: Well, we didn't use it all: who did?

LISTER: Aliens used our bog roll?

RIMMER: Just because they're aliens, doesn't mean they don't have to visit the little boys' room. Only they probably do something weird and alienesque – like it comes out of the top of their heads or something.

LISTER: I wouldn't like to be stuck behind one in a cinema.

They leave.

4. Int. R & R room. Day

The SKUTTERS *are playing some fairly funky keyboards. The* TOASTER *is doing bass vocals. The* CAT *has a microphone and is grooving in between them. He lifts the* MIC *to his lips and starts screeching a cat song.*

CAT: Eeeeeeh . . . Waaaaah . . . Mooo . . . Waaaaah . . . Eeeeeeh . . . hold it! Hold it!

SKUTTERS *stop.* TOASTER *keeps on doo-wopping.*

CAT: (*To* TOASTER) Hold it, bud. What are you doing?
TOASTER: I keep getting lost.
CAT: What you're doing, you're coming in too early. You're coming in on the "Eeeeeeh" when you should come in on the "Waaaah". You're making the whole thing sound stupid.
TOASTER: Maybe I should quit the band. I don't understand Cat music.
CAT: Look, it's simple. It's just a love song about a Cat pledging his affection for his lady Cat. It's called: 'I'll Love You, Babe, Until the Next Chick Comes Along'. Let's take it from the middle scream.

LISTER *and* RIMMER *come in.*

LISTER: Yo, Cat.
CAT: Hey, man, I'm rehearsing.
LISTER: There's something out there: we're getting a signal.
RIMMER: It's probably someone from another planet complaining about the music.

5. Int. Drive room. Day

HOLLY *is on a large monitor in the centre of the room.* LISTER, RIMMER *and* CAT *come in.* LISTER *has picked up a styrofoam cup of tea from a dispensing machine.*

HOLLY: It's a distress call, from a ship called the *Nova 5*. They've crash-landed. I'm trying to establish contact.

LISTER: Another ship! Brilliant.

RIMMER: It's not aliens, then?

HOLLY: No. They're from Earth. I hope they've got some spare odds and sods on board. We're a bit short of a few supplies.

RIMMER: Like what?

HOLLY: Cow's milk. We ran out of that yonks ago. Fresh *and* dehydrated.

LISTER: (*Sips tea*) What kind of milk are we using now then?

HOLLY: Emergency back-up supply. We're on the dog's milk.

LISTER *looks at his tea.*

LISTER: Dog's milk??

HOLLY: Nothing wrong with dog's milk. Full of goodness, full of vitamins, full of marrowbone jelly. Lasts longer than any other kind of milk, dog's milk.

LISTER: Why?

HOLLY: No bugger'll drink it. Plus, of course, the advantage of dog's milk is: when it's gone off, it tastes exactly the same as when it's fresh.

LISTER: Why didn't you tell me, man?

HOLLY: What? And put you off your tea?

LISTER *pours his tea into a bin.*

HOLLY: Hang about: we've got contact.

RIMMER: Punch it up.

On the screen: KRYTEN*'s face.*

KRYTEN: Thank goodness, thank goodness. Bless you! We were beginning to despair! Oh, forgive me. I'm Kryten, the service mechanoid aboard the *Nova 5*. We've had a terrible accident. Three male officers died on impact. The female officers are injured, but stable. Please help us.

CAT: Female? Is that female, as in soft and squidgy?

RIMMER: How many?

KRYTEN: Three. Miss Jane, Miss Tracy and Miss Anne. I am transmitting medical details.

Digitized pictures of three attractive women flash up. CAT *points at* RIMMER, *then* LISTER, *then himself.*

CAT: One, two, three . . .
LISTER: This is tremendous.

The CAT *shakes his finger at* RIMMER, *points at himself, then* LISTER, *then himself again.*

CAT: One, two, three . . .
LISTER: This is absolutely tremendous.

CAT *looks at* LISTER, *ruffles his brow, then points to himself three times:*

CAT: One, two, three! Can I handle it? Yes, I can.

RIMMER *turns away, smooths down his hair, then turns back to the screen as* KRYTEN *reappears.*

RIMMER: Tell them we're coming down to get them. By God, we'll rescue these fair blooms, or my name's not Captain A. J. Rimmer, Space Adventurer.
KRYTEN: Oh, thank you, Captain. Bless you.

The screen blanks.

LISTER: Space Adventurer?
RIMMER: What am I supposed to say: 'Fear not, I'm the bloke who used to clean the gunk out of the chicken soup machine? Actually, we know sod all about space travel, but if you've got a blocked nozzle, we're your lads.' That's going to fill them with confidence, that is.
LISTER: How far are we away, Hol?
HOLLY: About twenty-four hours.
CAT: Only twenty-four hours? I'd better start getting ready!

CAT *races off, pauses at door hatch:*

CAT: I'm so excited, all six of my nipples are tingling!
LISTER: What is wrong with him? This is a mercy mission. We're

taking them urgently needed medical supplies. We are not on the pull.

6. Int. Sleeping quarters. Day

LISTER *is getting ready to go out on the pull, grooving along to his ghetto blaster as he prepares his clothes. He is wearing off-white boxer shorts. His trousers are on the ironing-board. He is buffing his shoes with a cloth. Spit and buff. He's really doing a good job on these shoes. He finishes, then puts on the polishing cloth – it's his T-shirt. He grooves over to his locker and pulls out his single remaining clean sock. He tuts, bops over to the laundry basket and pulls out a very stiff, very smelly orange sock. He holds it at arm's length and sprays it with deodorant. He puts it on the ironing-board and hits it several times with a toffee hammer. He grooves over to the sink, picks up the toothpaste with his right hand, tosses it over to his left, picks up his toothbrush, squirts the paste in the air and starts brushing. He crosses to the ironing-board, picks up his trousers and puts them on. The iron has burnt a hole clean through to the right cheek. He grooves over to the locker, takes out a can of black spray paint and sprays the corresponding part of his boxer shorts.*

LISTER: Perfection.

RIMMER *comes in, sporting his dashing white official uniform, complete with his medals.*

RIMMER: Oh. You're not on the pull? Look at you: it's pathetic. You're wearing all your least smeggy things.

LISTER: Don't know what you're talking about.

RIMMER: That T-shirt with only the two curry stains on it: you only wear that on special occasions. You're toffed up to the nines.

LISTER: What about you. You look like Clive of India.

RIMMER: Oh, it's started. I knew it would.

LISTER: What has?

RIMMER: The put-downs. Always the same, whenever we meet girls. Put me down, and make yourself look good.

LISTER: Like when?

RIMMER: Remember those two little brunettes from Supplies? And I told them I worked in the stores, and they were very interested and asked me what I did there . . .

LISTER: And I said you were a shelf.

RIMMER: Right. And when I suggested a little trip to Titan zoo, you said: 'Oooh, he's taking you home to see his mum already.'

LISTER: So? They laughed.

RIMMER: Yes. At me. At my expense. Just don't put me down when we meet them.

LISTER: How d'you want me to act?

RIMMER: Just show a little respect. For a start, don't call me 'Rimmer'.

LISTER: Why not?

RIMMER: Because you always hit the '*Rim*' at the beginning. *Rim*mer. You make it sound like a lavatory disinfectant.

LISTER: Well, what should I call you? Rim*mer*?

RIMMER: I dunno. Arnie. Or Arn. Something a bit more . . . I dunno. How about 'Big Man'?

LISTER: Big Man??

RIMMER: Or the nickname I had at school.

LISTER: Bonehead?

RIMMER: How did you know my nickname was 'Bonehead'?

LISTER: I just guessed.

RIMMER: Well, I didn't mean that one. I meant the other one.

LISTER: Which one?

RIMMER: 'Ace'.

LISTER: Your nickname was never 'Ace'. Maybe 'Ace-hole'.

RIMMER: It was my nickname, actually. It's just, nobody ever called me it, no matter how many times I let them beat me up. I'm just saying: don't knock me down. Build me up.

LISTER: Like?

RIMMER: Like, if the chance occurs, and it comes up naturally in the conversation, perhaps you could mention I'm very brave.

LISTER: Do what?

RIMMER: Don't go ape. Just, you know, perhaps, when my back's turned, you could mention that I died, and I was, well, pretty incredibly brave about it.

LISTER *stares at him.*

RIMMER: Or . . . just kind of hint that I've had quite a few girlfriends.

LISTER *stares.*

RIMMER: Fine. Forget it. Just an idea. You're not wearing those boots, are you?
LISTER: Why? What's wrong with them?
RIMMER: They don't go. Not with that outfit. You should wear those dayglo orange moon boots.
LISTER: Eh? You said they were disgusting.
RIMMER: No. Very chic.
LISTER: You said they smelled like an orang-utan's posing pouch. You made me put them in the airlock.
RIMMER: No. They look terrific on you. I'd wear 'em.
LISTER: Honest?
RIMMER: Definitely.

7. Model shot
Wreck of Nova 5.

8. Int. Corridor, *Nova 5.* Dim
KRYTEN *is rushing down the sloping corridor.*

KRYTEN: Come on! They're here, everybody. They're in orbit. Heavens! There's so much to do.

He pauses to water a plant and carries on.

9. Int. Service deck, *Nova 5.* Day
KRYTEN *scurries in. Seated around the table are* THREE SKELETONS *with long hair, in* Nova 5 *uniforms.*

KRYTEN: Miss Jane! You haven't brushed your hair!

KRYTEN *starts combing a* SKELETON*'s hair.*

KRYTEN: What a mess you look.

He takes out some lipstick and applies it to the SKELETON.

KRYTEN: And Miss Anne – why haven't you touched your soup? It's no wonder you've started looking so pasty.

There is a creak, and Miss Anne's SKELETON *slumps head-first into her soup.*

KRYTEN: Eat nicely, Miss Anne. What on earth will the visitors think if they see you eating like that?

He goes up to the blonde SKELETON, *brandishing his hair brush.*

KRYTEN: Now then, Miss Tracy . . . (*Hesitates.*) No, you look absolutely perfect.

10. Model shot
Red Dwarf *in orbit over large asteroid.*

11. Int. *Blue Midget.* Space
Pan up from LISTER*'s vile orange moon boots.* RIMMER *is standing beside him, trying to pretend there's no stench.*

LISTER: (*Sniffs*) What's that smell?
RIMMER: I can't smell anything.
LISTER: Are you OK? Your eyes are watering.
RIMMER: Excitement. Look, we can't wait for the Cat. Let's just go.
LISTER: Come on: he's been preparing for a day and a night. Don't you want to see the result?

The CAT *comes in. He is wearing a gold space suit, like Armani would design, with a helmet two feet high and cone-shaped.*

CAT: I am a plastic surgeon's nightmare. Throw away the scalpel – improvements are impossible.

RIMMER: A space suit with cuff-links?

LISTER: Where'd you get that helmet?

CAT: Made it myself. Didn't want to muss up my hair. We just got to make sure we don't pass any mirrors, 'cause if we do, I'm there for the day.

HOLLY *appears on the monitor, wearing a toupee.*

HOLLY: All right? Everybody ready? Let's go, then.

LISTER: Holly, man: what are you doing?

HOLLY: What's wrong?

LISTER: The rug. Why are you wearing a toupee?

HOLLY: What toupee?

LISTER: The one on your head.

HOLLY: Whose head, then?

LISTER: Your head. You look like a gameshow host.

HOLLY: Oh. So it's not undetectable then. It doesn't blend in naturally and seamlessly with my own natural hair?

RIMMER: What is wrong with everybody? Three million years without a woman, and you all act like you're fourteen years old.

HOLLY: Oh, yeah? What about you and the socks?

LISTER: What socks?

RIMMER: Well, come on. We can't hang around . . .

HOLLY: He wanted two pairs of socks.

CAT: What for?

HOLLY: One pair to put on his feet, the other pair to roll up and put down his trousers.

RIMMER *crosses his legs. CUT TO:*

12. Int. Corridor, *Nova 5*. Day

KRYTEN *opens the airlock, and* LISTER, RIMMER *and the* CAT *step in.*

KRYTEN: Come in, come in. How lovely to meet you.

RIMMER: *Ĉarmita!* What a delightful craft. Reminds me of my first command.

KRYTEN: This way.

RIMMER *mouths to* LISTER: *'Ace, Ace'.* LISTER *pretends not to understand. They follow* KRYTEN. *They pass a mirror. The* CAT *catches sight of himself and freezes.*

CAT: You're a work of art, baby.

LISTER: Come on.

CAT: You're gonna have to help me.

LISTER *drags at* CAT, *who clings on to the mirror until he's torn away.*

CAT: Thanks, bud.

KRYTEN: I'm so excited. We all are. The girls could hardly stop themselves from jumping up and down.

RIMMER: (*Brays falsely*) Oh, Ĉarmita, ĉarmita.

KRYTEN: Ah! *Vi parolas esperanton, Kapitano Rimmer?*

RIMMER: Come again?

KRYTEN: You speak Esperanto, Captain Rimmer?

RIMMER: Oh, *si si si. Jawohl. Oui.*

13. Int. Service deck, *Nova 5*. Day

The SKELETONS, *as before.* KRYTEN *enters.*

KRYTEN: Well, here they are.

RIMMER *comes in and bows deeply.*

RIMMER: *Ĉarmita!*

He looks up. LISTER *and the* CAT *come in behind him. A long pause, as they all take in the view.*

LISTER: Well. It's difficult to know what to say, isn't it, Ace?

KRYTEN: Well, isn't anybody going to say 'Hello'?

LISTER: I think that little blonde one's giving you the eye.

KRYTEN: Now, you all get to know one another. I'll go and fetch some tea.

KRYTEN *waddles off. The* CAT *sits next to one of the* SKELETONS.

CAT: Hi, baby. What's happening? Did anyone ever tell you you have lovely eye sockets? Let's jump in a hot tub, we could make a great soup together.

RIMMER: I don't believe this.

LISTER: Be strong, Big Man.

RIMMER: Our one contact with intelligent life in three million and two years and he's the android equivalent of Norman Bates.

CAT: Come on, guys. So they're a little on the skinny side.

LISTER: (*To* SKELETONS) I know this may not be the time or the place to say this, but Ace here is incredibly brave.

RIMMER: Smeg off, dogfood face.

LISTER: And he's got just tons of girlfriends.

RIMMER: I'm warning you, Lister.

KRYTEN *returns with a tea-tray.*

KRYTEN: Is there something wrong?

RIMMER: Something wrong? They're dead.

KRYTEN: Who's dead?

RIMMER: (*Nods at* SKELETONS) *They're* dead. They're all dead.

KRYTEN: My God. I was only away two minutes.

RIMMER: They've been dead for centuries.

KRYTEN: No.

RIMMER: Yes.

KRYTEN: Are you a doctor?

RIMMER: You only have to look at them. They've got less meat on them than a chicken nugget!

KRYTEN: But what will I do? I'm programmed to serve them.

LISTER: Well, first thing, we should bury them.

KRYTEN: You're *that* sure they're dead?

RIMMER: Yes!

KRYTEN *goes over to the* BLONDE SKELETON.

KRYTEN: What about this one?

RIMMER: Well, there's a simple test. All right, girls. Hands up if you're alive.

KRYTEN *urges the* SKELETONS *to react. He is crestfallen when they do not.*

KRYTEN: What am I to do?

14. Model shot
Blue Midget *in space.*

15. Int. *Blue Midget.* Space
ALL *seated.* KRYTEN *at the back.*

KRYTEN: I can't leave them. Please, Mr David, please take me back.

LISTER: You've got to start a new life now.

KRYTEN: I don't have the software to cope with this. I was created to serve. I serve, therefore I am. That is my purpose: to serve and have no regard for myself.

LISTER: You're beginning to sound like my Auntie Mary.

KRYTEN: It's all I know.

LISTER: Well, you've got to change. You've got to work out what you want, Kryten, and stop being everybody's smegging doormat.

KRYTEN: That's easy for you to say. You're a human.

RIMMER: Only just.

16. Model shot
Red Dwarf *in space.*

17. Int. *Red Dwarf* corridor. Day
RIMMER *finds* KRYTEN *mooching in the corridor.*

RIMMER: Ah, Kryten! Nothing to do? Follow me.

18. Montage

KRYTEN *busying himself about the ship in various locations: simultaneously peeling potatoes and ironing clothes; painting walls; mopping floors; scrubbing skutters; consulting huge long list; turning pages for Rimmer in bed; polishing* HOLLY*'s monitor.*

19. Int. R & R room. Day

RIMMER *is lounging, reading a translucent shimmering book with a hologramatic 'H' on the spine.* KRYTEN *comes in, carrying a lightbox on which rests a small, translucent bell, also with an 'H' on it.*

RIMMER: Ah, Kryten. Have you completed the tasks I gave you?
KRYTEN: I've completed one hundred and seventy-five of them, sir.
RIMMER: So, you're not even a quarter of the way through.
KRYTEN: Here's the hologramatic bell you requested, sir.

RIMMER *takes the bell.*

RIMMER: Splendid. If I need anything, I'll ring for you.
KRYTEN: Thank you, Mr Arnold, sir.
RIMMER: Dismissed.

KRYTEN *bows and goes.* RIMMER *starts reading his book. He looks at the bell, picks it up and rings it.* KRYTEN *comes back.*

KRYTEN: Yes, Mr Arnold, sir?
RIMMER: Ah, Kryten: I don't want you for anything. I just wanted to check the bell was working.
KRYTEN: It is, sir.
RIMMER: Excellent. Dismiss.

KRYTEN *bows and goes.* RIMMER *rings the bell again.* KRYTEN *comes back.*

RIMMER: Ah, Kryten: you have absolutely no problem hearing the bell, then?
KRYTEN: None at all, Mr Arnold, sir.
RIMMER: Good. That'll be all.

KRYTEN *bows and goes.* RIMMER *rings the bell again.* KRYTEN *comes back.*

RIMMER: Kryten. I just wanted to say thanks for the bell. It's absolutely marvellous. I really am enjoying using it.

KRYTEN: Thank you, Mr Arnold, sir. Will that be all?

RIMMER: Yes. Carry on.

KRYTEN *bows and goes.* RIMMER *rings the bell again.* KRYTEN *comes back.*

RIMMER: Ah, Kryters: I don't want you for anything, I'm just wasting your time.

KRYTEN: Thank you, Mr Arnold, sir.

KRYTEN *bows and goes.*

RIMMER: I love this bell.

20. Int. Corridor, *Red Dwarf.* Day

LISTER *is bombing along on his souped-up shuttle bike, rock music blaring. He stops, turns off the music and listens. We hear a vacuum cleaner.*

LISTER: What is that noise? I've never heard that noise before. That is a *very* weird noise.

HOLLY: It's a vacuum cleaner, Dave.

LISTER: A vacuum leaner?

HOLLY: Cleaner. It's for cleaning floors.

LISTER: Is this a new thing?

21. Int. Sleeping quarters. Day

The quarters have been completely redecorated: tasteful, floral wallpaper; sash curtains over the porthole; draw curtains on the bunks; potted plants; nice rugs; a pine table and chairs. The table is covered in newly polished boots and piles of neatly folded fresh laundry. KRYTEN *is vacuuming the rug.* LISTER *walks in. Vacuum off.*

LISTER: What the smeg is going on?

KRYTEN: Good afternoon, Mr David, sir.

LISTER *picks up some freshly laundered boxers.*

LISTER: What are these?

KRYTEN: Your boxer shorts, Mr David.

LISTER: No way are these my boxer shorts. They *bend*. What have you done to this place?

KRYTEN: I've done a spot of tidying up.

LISTER: Where is everything? Where's my coffee mug with the mould in it?

KRYTEN: I threw it away, sir.

LISTER: You what? I was breeding that mould. He was called 'Albert'. I was trying to get him two feet high.

KRYTEN: Why, sir?

LISTER: Because it drove Rimmer nuts, and driving Rimmer nuts is what keeps me going.

KRYTEN: I'm sorry Mr David.

LISTER: And stop calling me 'Mr David'. It makes it sound like I'm better than you.

KRYTEN: But you are better than me. You're a human being.

LISTER: Hey, listen: some of the worst people I ever met were human beings. My French teacher was officially classed as a human being. It doesn't mean anything.

KRYTEN: Whatever you say, sir.

LISTER: What's wrong with you? Why are you doing all this.

KRYTEN: Serving makes me happy, sir.

LISTER: What about *you*? Don't you ever want to do anything just for yourself?

KRYTEN: Myself?? That's a bit of a barmy notion, if you don't mind my saying so, sir.

LISTER: Come on. There must be something. What do you look forward to?

KRYTEN: (*Thinks*) *Androids*. (*He sings a few bars of the theme music.*)

LISTER: That stupid soap opera? Why?

KRYTEN: Because for half an hour a week, I can forget I'm me.

LISTER: What else?

KRYTEN: Being asleep.

LISTER: *Androids* and being asleep. Sounds like a crazy, fun-packed life you've got there, Kryten.

KRYTEN: I have strange thoughts when I'm asleep.

LISTER: Yeah. They're called 'dreams'.

KRYTEN: I'm in a garden – I've never seen a garden, except in books – and I've planted everything, and helped it to grow. It's my garden, and there's no one there but me. Just me and all the plants I made live. Silly.

LISTER: So, do it. Find a planet with an atmosphere and do it.

KRYTEN: I can't. I'm programmed to serve.

LISTER: But there's no one *to* serve. That's all over now.

KRYTEN: What about Mr Arnold. I've got to complete all the tasks he set me.

LISTER: Rimmer told you to do all this?

KRYTEN: Mr Arnold is my new master now.

LISTER: Mr Arnold is not his name. His name is Rimmer. Or smeghead. Or dinosaur breath. Or molecule mind. And on the very rare occasion when you want to be really mega-polite to him, you may, in those exceptional circumstances, call him buttsuck.

22. Model shot. *Red Dwarf* in space

23. Int. Sleeping quarters. Day

The CAT *helps himself to some soup from a large tureen.* LISTER *is reading a zero G football magazine on his bunk.* RIMMER *is posing in his white uniform while* KRYTEN *paints his portrait.*

RIMMER: I think it'll be best on this wall, sort of dominating the room.

KRYTEN: Yes, Mr Arnold.

RIMMER: And have you built the oak frame for it yet?

KRYTEN: Yes, Mr Arnold.

LISTER: (*Mimics*) 'Yes, Mr Arnold'. You're a total gimp, Kryten. You know that?

KRYTEN: Yes, Mr David.

LISTER: 'Yes, Mr David'.

RIMMER: Leave it alone, Lister. It likes doing all my little jobs. It makes it happy.

LISTER: Oh, drop dead, Rimmer.

RIMMER: Already have done.

LISTER: Encore.

CAT: You'd never get a cat to be a servant. Ever see a cat return a stick? 'Hey, bud, you threw the stick, go get it yourself! You want the stick so bad, why'd you throw it away in the first place?'

LISTER: You didn't get anything from those movies, did you?

RIMMER: What movies?

KRYTEN: Mr David was kind enough to take me to see *The Wild Ones*, *Easy Rider*, and *Rebel without a Cause*.

LISTER: Thought it might do him some good. Fat chance. Middle of Brando's rebel speech, he gets out a brush-o-matic and starts doing my lapels.

RIMMER: Well, perhaps now you'll learn, Lister: there's a natural order to things. Some give orders, others obey. That's the way it's always been, and that's the way it always will be. Isn't that true, Kryten?

KRYTEN: Yes, Mr Arnold.

LISTER: Oh, what's the point?

KRYTEN: I've finished, Mr Arnold.

RIMMER: Excellent.

RIMMER *crosses to the portrait. We see it as* RIMMER *sees it: the painted Rimmer is sitting, looking extremely pompous, but instead of a chair, he's on a toilet, and his trousers are down by his ankles.* RIMMER *looks at the painting.* RIMMER *looks at* KRYTEN. KRYTEN *looks at* RIMMER.

KRYTEN: It's rather good, isn't it?

RIMMER *looks at the painting.*

RIMMER: (*Quietly*) What are you doing?

KRYTEN *looks at the painting, dabs it with his brush.*

KRYTEN: I think . . . I'm rebelling.
RIMMER: (*Quietly*) Rebelling.
KRYTEN: I think that's what I'm doing.
RIMMER: You're rebelling?
KRYTEN: . . . Yes.
RIMMER: What are you rebelling against?
KRYTEN: (*Brando*) Whaddaya got?

KRYTEN *picks up the soup tureen and empties it all over* RIMMER*'s bunk. He flicks* RIMMER *the bird:*

KRYTEN: Swivel on it, punk.

He exchanges high fives with LISTER.

KRYTEN: I need your bike.
LISTER: You got it.

KRYTEN *swaggers out.*

RIMMER: Where's he going.
LISTER: I think he's going gardening.

RIMMER *looks baffled.*

24. Int. Cargo Bay. Day
KRYTEN *climbs on to* LISTER*'s space bike, wearing a leather jacket and a* Brando Wild Ones *cap. He revs up, soars off and we:*

Run credits

ME²

1. Model shot. *Red Dwarf* in space

2. Int. Sleeping quarters. Day

LISTER *is packing* RIMMER*'s things into a trunk. He picks up a book and reads the title:*

LISTER: *The Pop-up Kama Sutra – Zero Gravity Edition.* That's mine.

LISTER *throws the book on his bed, with some others. He picks up another.*

LISTER: (*Reads*) *Astronavigation and Invisible Numbers in Engineering Structure Made Simple.* Rimmer's.

He tosses the book into the trunk and picks up a video cassette. RIMMER *comes in.*

LISTER: *Arnold J. Rimmer – A Tribute.* What's this?
RIMMER: It's a video of my death. Holly made it up for me.
LISTER: You're very strange, Rimmer.
RIMMER: What's so strange? You have videos of weddings and births.
LISTER: So what d'you do? Have a few friends round, give 'em a sherry and invite 'em to watch you snuff it?
RIMMER: My death, Lister, is one of the most important things that ever happened to me. Just stick it in the trunk and shut up.
LISTER: Weird.
RIMMER: What about these posters?

136

LISTER: They're mine.

RIMMER: I know they're yours. But the Blu-tack's mine.

LISTER: You want to take the Blu-tack?

RIMMER: Well, it is mine. I did pay for it. With my money.

LISTER: I think there's one of your old toenail clippings under the bed. I'll put that in too, shall I?

RIMMER: This is the best decision I ever made. It's the dawn of a new age for me, matey-pie. No more you, with your stupid, annoying face, and your stupid, annoying habits. No more you, holding me back, dragging me down.

LISTER: Me? How did I hold you back?

RIMMER: Oh, all kinds of ways: swapping my toothpaste with a tube of spermicidal jelly . . .

LISTER: That was a joke!

RIMMER: Yes, on me, at my expense.

LISTER: Rimmer, you can't blame me for having a lousy life.

RIMMER: Oh yes I can.

LISTER: It's always the same: you never had the right set of pens for G&E drawing. Your dividers don't stretch far enough . . .

RIMMER: Well they don't.

LISTER: In the end, you can't turn round and say: 'Sorry I buggered up my life, it was all Lister's fault.'

RIMMER: Well, I'm not, am I? I'm moving out. Out of slob city and into successville.

LISTER: You mean next door?

RIMMER: It's not the place, it's the company. Sharing my life with someone who'll give me encouragement, understanding, help. The thrust and parry of meaningful conversation.

RIMMER 2 *pops his head round the door. He is identical, except he is wearing a slightly different-coloured uniform from* RIMMER*'s.*

RIMMER 2: Everything tickety-boo?

RIMMER: *Absolument.* I'll be along lickety-split.

The TWO RIMMERS *exchange full single-Rimmer salutes.*

RIMMER 2: Carry on.

They salute again. RIMMER 2 *goes.*

RIMMER: What a guy. I don't know why I didn't think of this before: a duplicate me.

LISTER *picks up a large plant.*

LISTER: Is this yours?
RIMMER: It's nice, isn't it? Of course it's mine.

3. Int. Corridor. Day
LISTER *walks along the corridor with the plant and turns into Rimmer's new quarters. He stops and reads the sign on the door: 'Second Technician Arnold J. Rimmer and Second Technician Arnold J. Rimmer'. He shakes his head and goes into:*

4. Int. The Rimmers' quarters. Day
RIMMER 2 *is supervising a skutter unpacking a box.*

RIMMER 2: Ah, Lister: stick it on the locker by the revision timetable.
LISTER: Why have you got the 'No Smoking' sign up, when neither of you smoke?
RIMMER 2: Because it's my 'No Smoking' sign, and I happen to think it looks rather striking.

LISTER *spots a collection of cut-out newspaper headlines on the noticeboard.*

LISTER: (*Reads*) 'Arnold does it best', 'Arnold's tops with us!', 'I owe it all to Rimmer' . . . that's very funny stuff.
RIMMER 2: Just go.
LISTER: Because, like, your name's Rimmer, and even though these headlines are about other people, you've cut them out, put them on your wall, and people will think they're about you.

RIMMER 2: Shoo, shoo. Go on.

LISTER: This joke could keep me laughing all through the winter.

RIMMER 2: I don't have to take this anymore. I don't have to put up with your snide remarks, your total slobbiness, your socks that set off the sprinkler system. Kindly vacate our new quarters.

LISTER *mimics the Rimmer salute and goes.*

5. Int. Corridor. Day

Deserted. From a locker against the hull, the CAT *emerges, looks around and turns up his collar.*

CAT: Hey – nobody is going to find *that* one.

He slinks off down the corridor, carrying a bottle of champagne and a megaphone.

CAT: Hey, I'm slinking good today. Was slinking bad last week. Funny how you can just lose it.

He raises the megaphone.

CAT: (*Into the megaphone*) Hello, hello, testing. One, one, one, me, me, me. Hello: can anyone hear me? I am feeling horny. I repeat: horny. I need sex very badly. Can you hear me? Horny cat requires sex. This is an emergency.

6. Int. Drive room. Day

LISTER *is watching a Mugs Murphy cartoon on the viewscreen. Off, we hear the* CAT *through his megaphone.*

CAT: (*Off*) Attention all lady cats. Can you hear me?

LISTER: Hold.

The cartoon freezes.

CAT: (*Off*) Sensual emergency! Good loving needed bad!

The CAT *enters, takes two steps, falls effortlessly into a roll and pops up still clutching the megaphone and champagne.*

CAT: No girls here. What a waste of a good roll.

LISTER: Hi, Cat, I've been looking for you.

CAT *puts down the champagne and megaphone, takes out his little steam iron and starts pressing his jacket.*

CAT: Shame, I'm looking so good, too.

LISTER: Listen: Rimmer's moved out, and I thought it'd be brilliant if you moved in with me.

CAT: With you? In your place?

LISTER: Yeah.

CAT: I'd rather live upside-down in a toilet bowl.

LISTER: It'll be great. We'll have a few laughs.

CAT: Why would I move in with you? I want to be on my own. I like me. I will not hurt me, I will not steal from me, I will not jump on me when I'm not in the mood.

LISTER: Come on, it'll be company. Life's nicer when you share.

CAT: 'Share'? What is 'share'?

LISTER: Share is when a person has something and he lets another person use it.

CAT: Oh right. There's a Cat word for that. We don't say 'share', we say 'stupid'. As in: 'look what the stupid person gave me'.

LISTER: Come on: what d'you say?

CAT: I say . . .

Picks up megaphone and exits, calling:

CAT: (*Through megaphone*) Hello, lady cats: baby-maker requires work . . . prepared to work long hours . . . hello, hello . . .

7. Model shot. *Red Dwarf* in space
Over, we hear:

RIMMER: Up, up, up . . .

RIMMER 2: Stretch, stretch, stretch . . .

8. Int. The Rimmers' quarters. Night

The TWO RIMMERS *are exercising in front of their bunks, in shorts and vests.*

RIMMER: Come on. Keep it up.

RIMMER 2: And you. You keep it up, too.

RIMMER: Jump higher.

RIMMER 2: Stretch further.

RIMMER: Faster

RIMMER 2: Faster still.

RIMMER: And rest.

RIMMER *stops.*

RIMMER 2: No, no. Keep it going.

RIMMER *starts up again.*

RIMMER: You're right, you're right. Keep it going.

RIMMER 2: And rest.

They both stop.

RIMMER: Brilliant. That little bit extra. That's what it's all about.

RIMMER 2: I drive and encourage you . . .

RIMMER: And I drive and encourage you.

RIMMER 2: And I drive and encourage you.

RIMMER: Have you done tomorrow's Daily Goal List?

RIMMER 2: No, I haven't.

RIMMER: Well, do it. Now! Come on. Chop, chop.

RIMMER 2: Right away. Absolutely. Have you done yours?

RIMMER: Not yet. I was just going to . . .

RIMMER 2: That's not good enough.

RIMMER: You're right. You're absolutely right, Arnold: I'll do it immediately.

RIMMER 2: OK, what time shall we get up?

RIMMER: Early. Half-past eight.

RIMMER 2: No, earlier than that. Seven.

RIMMER: How about six?

RIMMER 2: No! Half-past four!

RIMMER: Half-past four? That's the middle of the night.

RIMMER 2: You wanted to be driven – I'm driving you.

RIMMER: Once again, you're absolutely right. Holly, alarm call: four-thirty in the morning. Make it the sonic boom, extra loud emergency one.

HOLLY: Yes, Arnolds.

RIMMER 2 *climbs on to his bunk*.

RIMMER 2: You know, Holly was saying, if we could tap into another power source, we could run off thousands of copies of us.

RIMMER: Like bootleg cassettes.

RIMMER 2: The whole ship could be populated with Rimmers.

RIMMER: A whole planet.

HOLLY: Yeah. Trouble with that is: if ever you had a party, no one would bring any booze.

RIMMER: Shut up, Holly.

RIMMER 2: Yes, that's a double order: shut up, Holly.

RIMMER *climbs on to his bunk*.

RIMMER 2: What are you doing?

RIMMER: Going to bed, Arnold.

RIMMER 2: Look, it's barely midnight. You could get in a couple of hours of revision.

RIMMER: But I'm getting up in a minute.

RIMMER 2: You wanted to be driven: I'm driving you.

RIMMER: You're right! You're right! You take porous circuits and Esperanto, I'll take thermal energy and the history of philosophy.

RIMMER 2: This is heaven. We're being pushed. We're being driven.

RIMMER: Better than sex!

9. Int. Sleeping quarters. Night

The screen is filled with an enormous pink bubble gum bubble. A pair of dividers comes into shot to measure it. PULL OUT. It's LISTER blowing the bubble. He measures the dividers against the bubble and writes down the result.

LISTER: (*Writing*) Ten and three-quarter centimetres. Plus five for not bursting. That is a big score. The blues have got to do something quite sensational with their last bubble. Quiet please. Chew on.

He puts down the pink gum and pops some chewed blue gum into his mouth.

LISTER: (*Chewing*) And they're off to a good start. Come on, you blues! And here comes the bubble. And it feels like a big one.

HOLLY *appears on the monitor.*

HOLLY: Bored, Dave?

The bubble bursts on LISTER's face.

LISTER: No.
HOLLY: Well I bloody am.

LISTER *spots a cassette lying half under the bunk. He picks it up.*

LISTER: Look at this: Rimmer's death video. Get me some popcorn and stick the video on, would you, Hol?
HOLLY: I can just about manage that, yes.

LISTER *pops the cassette into the VCR. The TV flicks on, and we move into the screen. A black border and, framed in a floral motif, the caption:* 'A Tribute to Arnold J. Rimmer, BSC, SSC'

HOLLY: (*VO*) 'BSC'? 'SSC'? What's that?
LISTER: Bronze swimming certificate, silver swimming certificate.

The HOLOGRAM RIMMER appears on-screen. Beneath him, the caption: 'Arnold Rimmer (Deceased)'.

RIMMER: This video pays homage to a man who fell short of greatness by a gnat's wing. Before this digitized recording of his final moments, there will be a lengthy tribute, interspersed with poetry readings, read by me.

LISTER: Spin on.

The picture spins on, then plays:

RIMMER: . . . and if it hadn't been for those people holding him back, dragging him down . . .

LISTER: Spin on.

The picture spins on, then plays:

RIMMER: . . . what I'm basically saying is: if you'd put Napoleon in quarters with Lister, he'd probably still be in Corsica, peeling spuds.

LISTER: On!

The picture spins on, then plays:

RIMMER: . . . the final moments of Arnold J. Rimmer.

On-screen, a slightly pixilized version of the following scene:

10. PRE-VT. Int. Drive room. Day

Just before the accident. The LIVE RIMMER *is getting a dressing-down from the* CAPTAIN.

CAPTAIN: It was your *job* to fix it, Rimmer. You can't do sloppy work on drive plates!

RIMMER: I know, sir, and I accept full responsibility for any consequences.

There is a huge roar, growing louder and louder as the explosion rips through the ship towards the drive room. RIMMER *turns to look where the noise is coming from.*

SLO-MO: RIMMER *and the* CAPTAIN *are blown to the floor by the wind preceding the explosion.* RIMMER, *in echo, utters his last words:*

RIMMER: Gazpacho soup . . .

*SLO-MO: a glass paperweight (*Red Dwarf *in a dust storm) falls from the captain's desk and shatters in front of* RIMMER*'s outstretched hand.*

There is a blinding white flash, and when the screen clears, RIMMER *and the* CAPTAIN *are now just two piles of white dust. Back to live action:*

LISTER: Off! Gazpacho soup? Why were his last words 'Gazpacho soup'?

11. Model shot. *Red Dwarf* in space
Over, we hear:

HOLLY: (*VO*) It's four-thirty: here is your early-morning alarm call.

A huge sonic boom explosion, followed by the two RIMMERS *screaming:*

RIMMER & RIMMER 2: Off! Off! Off!

12. Int. Corridor. Morning
RIMMER *is supervising the skutter painting the corridor.*

RIMMER: That bit! You've missed that bit. And this bit here. No, no, do that bit and then do this bit.

He turns and raises his voice in the direction of LISTER*'s door.*

RIMMER: That's it! That's the way. Smooth and even. Up and down.

Lister's door opens. A sleepy LISTER *pokes his head out.*

RIMMER: Ah! Lister. Bonnus matinola. Didn't wake you, I trust?
LISTER: What are you doing, Rimmer?
RIMMER: Painting the corridor. Changing it from ocean grey to military grey. Something that should have been done a long time ago.

LISTER: Looks the same to me.

RIMMER: Nonsense. This is all the new bit here, and that's the dowdy old nasty ocean grey bit there.

RIMMER *peers at the wall.*

RIMMER: Or is it the other way around?

LISTER: It's six o'clock in the morning.

RIMMER: That late, eh? Almost time for lunch.

LISTER: Lunch?

RIMMER: Some of us have been up and about for some considerable time. Getting things done. Achieving things.

LISTER: Yeah, well, can you achieve 'em more quietly?

LISTER *turns to go.*

RIMMER: And while I'm doing this, my other self is busy collating all the drive reports, then he revises engineering, I revise Esperanto, we meet, test each other, then he's off to shampoo the seats in the cinema, while I check all the circuit covers, then it's time to get down to the main work of the day.

HOLLY: Arnold, you asked me to remind you when it's time for your Esperanto revision.

RIMMER: Thank you, Holly. (*To* SKUTTER) You, carry on.

RIMMER *marches off smartly.* LISTER *waits for a second, then heads for Rimmer's room.*

13. Int. The Rimmers' quarters. Morning

There are two new signs: 'You don't have to have a rather dry sense of humour to live here, but it certainly helps!' and 'Tomorrow is the first day of the rest of your death'.

  LISTER *enters furtively. He scans the bookcase and finally finds what he's looking for. He pulls out a book,* 'The A to Z of Red Dwarf', *opens it, and takes out a slim volume concealed within:* 'My Diary – Arnold J. Rimmer'. *He flicks through the pages and stops on the 15th of March – a page with a black border drawn around it and, in sombre writing,* 'Gazpacho Day'.

Suddenly Rimmer's locker opens and the CAT *emerges with his back to* LISTER.

CAT: He won't find that one till he changes his boots.

The CAT *spots* LISTER, *holds his hands over his face and starts backing out.*

CAT: Did you see him clearly? Did you get a good look at his face? Could you spot him in a parade? I don't think so. I could have been anybody.

14. Int. Lister's quarters. Morning

LISTER *enters with a can of beer.*

LISTER: Holly, give me a punch up of ship journal recording 15th March, year of the accident. I want to follow Rimmer through the day.
HOLLY: The whole of that day's recording has been erased.
LISTER: All of it?
HOLLY: It was erased by Rimmer.
LISTER: What the hell's gazpacho soup got to do with anything?

15. Int. The Rimmers' quarters. Day

RIMMER *enters, looking totally exhausted. He sits on the bed, groans and stretches.*

RIMMER: Look, Holly, I think I may have a quick nap for ten minutes or so. Can you wake me up in two hours?
HOLLY: Yes, Arnold, I'll put that on your Goal List. New item 3: sleep all day.
RIMMER: Shut up.

RIMMER *lies back, thankfully, and closes his eyes.* RIMMER 2 *comes in, equally exhausted. He sees the supine* RIMMER *and gets a new burst of energy.*

RIMMER 2: What are you doing?

147

RIMMER: (*Eyes still closed*) . . . and, in conclusion, we have seen throughout this essay how very important, nay, essential, invisible numbers are in engineering structures.

RIMMER *leaps off the bunk.*

RIMMER: Oh, hi, Arnie. (*Gives Rimmer salute.*) On to item numbero five. Can't hang about.

RIMMER 2: You were having a nap, weren't you?

RIMMER: No, I was doing an essay.

RIMMER 2: The old 'pretending to finish an essay' routine won't work with me, miladdo.

RIMMER: No, I was. Honestly. Truly.

RIMMER 2: You're forgetting – I *am* you.

RIMMER: I swear the most sacred oath, on my mother's eyes.

RIMMER 2: You can't lie to me.

RIMMER: You're right – I was lying.

RIMMER 2: What is the point of getting up at four-thirty and then going to bed halfway through the morning?

RIMMER: You're right, you're right.

RIMMER 2: You wanted to be driven.

RIMMER: I did, I did . . .

RIMMER 2: Then get out there and on to the next item.

They salute.

RIMMER: Thank you.

RIMMER *goes.* RIMMER 2 *sits on the bunk, stretches out and groans.* RIMMER *returns.*

RIMMER: Hang on. What are you doing in here?

RIMMER 2: . . . and, in summation, the Laws of Thermodynamics . . . You're right, you're right.

RIMMER: You can't fool me, and I can't fool you. On to the next item. Push yourself.

RIMMER 2: Through the pain barrier.

RIMMER & RIMMER 2: (*Together, weakly*) Fantastic.

As they both turn to leave, we see behind their backs: they are secretly flicking V-signs at each other.

16. Model shot. *Red Dwarf* in space

17. Int. Lister's quarters. Night.
LISTER *is asleep on the top bunk. Vaguely we can make out voices. The noise wakes* LISTER. *Gradually increasing in clarity, we hear the* TWO RIMMERS *having a blazing row.*

RIMMER: (*VO*) Oh, that's charming!

RIMMER 2: (*VO*) Shut up. Lister will hear you.

RIMMER: (*VO*) I make you vomit?

RIMMER 2: (*VO*) Keep your voice down.

RIMMER: (*VO*) You wanted driving, didn't you?

RIMMER 2: (*VO*) Yes, but you're driving me crazy.

RIMMER: (*VO*) It's no wonder you never made anything of your life. No wonder you're a complete and total failure.

RIMMER 2: (*VO*) You've got a really nasty side to your nature. It's no wonder Father never loved you.

RIMMER: (*VO*) That's a lie. A lie lie lie lie lie lie lie!

RIMMER 2: (*VO*) Then why did he never send you to the Academy?

RIMMER: (*VO*) He couldn't afford it.

RIMMER 2: (*VO*) He sent all your brothers.

RIMMER: (*VO*) You filthy smegging lying smegging liar.

RIMMER 2: (*VO: sing-song*) Daddy didn't love you, Daddy didn't love you . . .

RIMMER: (*VO*) Mummy didn't love you, Mummy didn't love you . . .

RIMMER 2: (*VO*) Oh that is the pits, that really is. It's not that she didn't love me. She was just . . . busy.

RIMMER: (*VO*) Face facts, Rimsey baby – you can't cut it, you never have been able to cut it, and you never will be able to cut it.

RIMMER 2: (*VO*) Well, that's rich, coming from you: Mr Gazpacho!

Total silence. LISTER*'s eyes widen. Still silence. More silence.*

RIMMER: (*VO*) Mr What?

RIMMER 2: (*VO*) You heard.

RIMMER: (*VO*) I don't believe I did. Because if you said what I think you said . . .

RIMMER 2: (*VO*) I said: 'Mr GAZPACHO', deafie!!

RIMMER: (*VO*) That is the most obscenely hurtful thing . . .

RIMMER 2: (*VO*) Good!!

RIMMER: (*VO*) That's the straw that broke the dromedary, that is. You're finished, Rimmer.

RIMMER 2: (*VO*) No, *you're* finished, Rimmer.

We hear boots stomping down the corridor. Lister's door opens and RIMMER *enters, in his space corps pyjamas.*

RIMMER: Ah, Lister. How are you?

LISTER: Hi. What d'you want?

RIMMER: Uh, I uh . . . I don't suppose you've managed to get all that Blu-tack together for me?

LISTER: Rimmer, it's three in the morning.

RIMMER: Doesn't matter. It can wait till tomorrow.

RIMMER *climbs on to his bunk.*

RIMMER: I'll sleep here till you're ready. Goodnight.

LISTER: Everything all right, is it?

RIMMER: For sure. Absolutely.

LISTER: No problems, then?

RIMMER: No, no. Things couldn't be much hunky-dorier.

LISTER: So, you weren't having a blazing row?

RIMMER: What? That's quite an amusing thought, isn't it? Having a blazing row with yourself.

From next door we hear RIMMER 2:

RIMMER 2: (*VO*) Hit the wall! Go on, hit the wall!

We hear a skutter hitting the wall.

RIMMER 2: (*VO: shouts*) Can you shut up, Rimmer? Some of us are trying to sleep!!

RIMMER: I mean, obviously, we have professional disagreements, but nothing malicious. Nothing with any side to it.

RIMMER 2: (*VO: screeching*) Shut up, you dead git!!!

RIMMER: (*Calmly*) Excuse me.

He crosses to the door and shouts down the corridor:

RIMMER: Stop your foul whining, you filthy piece of rectal cancer.

He comes back in.

RIMMER: Look, it's pointless concealing it. Rimmer and me, well . . . we've had a bit of a tiff. It goes without saying it was his fault.

18. Model shot. *Red Dwarf* in space
Over, we hear cinema advertising music.

19. Int. Ship's cinema. Day
LISTER *is making a pig of himself with a sauce-laden hot dog, a slurpy drink, popcorn and a cigarette. Beside him, the* CAT *looks suitably disgusted. On the screen, Indian music with various stills.*

VO: Miles from Earth, deep in the heart of the solar system, and you fancy a curry? Then why not drop in at the Titan Taj Mahal Indian restaurant. Enjoy the finest tandoori cuisine and one-fifth gravity. Just a short space walk from this cinema . . .

LISTER *pigs noisily. The* CAT *raises his megaphone to Lister's ear and shouts:*

CAT: Shut . . . up!!!

LISTER: Don't keep doing that!

CAT: (*Through megaphone*) I'm trying to watch the movie.

LISTER: I'm just eating.

CAT: No. Eating is when food goes in your *mouth*.

RIMMER *walks down the aisle.*

RIMMER: Afternoon.

RIMMER *sits next to* LISTER.

RIMMER: What's on?

LISTER: *Citizen Kane.*

RIMMER: There's no smoking on this side. You should be sitting over there.

LISTER: No one's complaining.

RIMMER: I am. So would you kindly move to the proper designated smoking area?

LISTER: I thought you hated films.

RIMMER: Yes, I do.

LISTER: Why are you here? Where's Mrs Rimmer?

RIMMER: Don't ask me. He's nothing to do with me. Last time I saw him, he was re-doing my paintwork: changing it from military grey back to ocean grey. He's quite, quite mad.

CAT: (*Through megaphone*) Would you like to shut up?

RIMMER: You only have to be with him five seconds and he drives you mad. Look, put that out or move.

RIMMER 2 *comes down the aisle.*

RIMMER 2: (*Nodding hello*) Lister, Cat.

He takes the seat in front of RIMMER. *Cruddy organ music starts up.*

RIMMER: Excuse me, I can't see.

RIMMER 2: Shhhh!

RIMMER: Excuse me, I can't see through the back of your stupid, curly-haired sticky-out-eared head.

LISTER: Guys, I'm trying to watch the film.

RIMMER: Move!

RIMMER 2: Look, I just happened to choose a seat, purely at random. If you're unhappy with your seat, I suggest you move.

RIMMER: Right.

RIMMER stands and starts pretending to look for a seat.

RIMMER: Shall I sit here? No. Here? No. Ah! There's a nice-looking one.

He sits directly in front of RIMMER 2.

RIMMER 2: (*Sighs*) Look at this. Mr Maturity.

RIMMER 2 gets up and sits in front of RIMMER.

LISTER: Will you two just grow up?
RIMMER: Two? I think there's only one immature person here. And I think we all know who it is.

RIMMER gets up and sits in front of RIMMER 2.

RIMMER 2: I'm not participating in this pathetic farce any longer. We'll see who's mature.

RIMMER 2 gets up.

RIMMER 2: Enjoy your film.

RIMMER 2 goes off. We see the screen. The film starts. Suddenly it is obscured by a huge silhouette hand rabbit. CAT *and* LISTER *exchange despairing looks. SHOT:* RIMMER 2 *making shadow puppets in the light streaming from the projector. Back to the screen. The rabbit changes into two fingers flicking the Vs.* LISTER *stands.*

LISTER: Look, this can't go on. One of yous has got to go.
RIMMER & RIMMER 2: (*Together*) Yes. Him.
RIMMER: Look, it's crystal smegging clear which one of us has got to go.
RIMMER 2: Yes, you.
RIMMER: Look, I was here first. I nursed Listy through the early days.
RIMMER 2: We're identical. We're exactly the same person, only you're mentally unstable.
LISTER: (*Pointing as he recites*): Ippy, dippy,

My space shippy,
On a course so true,
Past old Neptune,
And Pluto's moon,
The one I choose is you.

He ends on RIMMER.

RIMMER 2: Excellent. Excellent decision. Turn him off.
RIMMER: And the one you end on is the one who stays, yes?
LISTER: Rimmer, it's you.
RIMMER: But I was here first!
RIMMER 2: Stop bleating. Get it over with. Turn him off.
RIMMER: Wait a minute, wait a minute. At least give me some time to prepare myself.
LISTER: Drive room, ten minutes.
RIMMER: I can't believe it. I've been ippy-dippied to death.
RIMMER 2: But, in a sense, aren't we all ippy-dippied to death? What a fascinating thought. And one Lister and I can discuss this evening, after you no longer exist.

20. Int. Drive room. Day

LISTER *takes a swig from a whisky bottle. The* CAT *is napping.* RIMMER 2 *is seated, smiling in anticipation.*

LISTER: I want you out.
RIMMER 2: What have I said?
LISTER: Out.

RIMMER 2 *gets up, shaking his head.*

RIMMER 2: There's precious little entertainment on this ship. If you can't attend the odd execution, what've you got left?

21. Int. Corridor. Day

RIMMER, *freshly shaved, wearing a dashing white naval-esque uniform, with four gleaming medals on his breast, is marching down the corridor.* RIMMER 2 *passes him, looks and shakes his head.* RIMMER *marches on to:*

22. Int. Drive room. Day

He stops and salutes.

RIMMER: Lister.

LISTER: Listen – I'm not enjoying this . . .

RIMMER: There's nothing to say. Let's get on with it.

LISTER: Have a drink.

RIMMER *shakes his head.*

LISTER: I didn't know you had any medals.

RIMMER *shrugs.*

LISTER: What are they?

RIMMER *taps the medals in succession.*

RIMMER: Three years' long service, six years' long service, nine years' long service and, uh . . . (*as if remembering*) twelve years' long service.

LISTER: Come on. One drink.

RIMMER: I'll have a whisky.

HOLLY: How would you like it?

RIMMER: Straight. (*BEAT*) With ice and lemonade. (*BEAT*) And a slice of lemon. (*BEAT*) And a cherry.

RIMMER *twitches as Holly simulates a slug of whisky.*

LISTER: Another?

RIMMER *nods. BEAT. He twitches again.*

RIMMER: Another.

Twitches again.

RIMMER: And another womb. Make it a double.

RIMMER *twitches, shudders, twitches, shudders. He flops on to a seat and runs his hands through his hair.*

RIMMER: (*Sighs*) Ahhhhh. I was no good at life. I was no good at death. And now I'm going to die again. D'you want to know my greatest night? The greatest night of my life. It was when I was invited to the Captain's table. I'd only been with the company five years. Six officers and me. They called me Arnold.

RIMMER *shakes his fist triumphantly.*

RIMMER: We had gazpacho soup for starters. I didn't know gazpacho soup was meant to be cold. I called over Chen and told him to take it away and bring it back hot. He did. The looks on their faces still haunt me today. I thought they were laughing at Chen, and all the time they were laughing at me, as I ate my piping hot gazpacho soup. That was the last time I ate at the Captain's table. That was the end of my career.

LISTER: Is that it? That's the whole gazpacho soup business?

RIMMER: If only they'd mentioned it at basic training. Instead of climbing up and down ropes and crawling through tunnels on your elbows. If just once they'd said: 'Gazpacho soup is served cold', I could have been an admiral now. Instead of a nothing, which is what I am, let's face it.

LISTER: You're not a nothing.

CAT: (*Eyes still closed*) He is.

RIMMER: You're right.

CAT: I know I'm right.

RIMMER: I never got off the bottom rung. You know why? Because I didn't have the right parents. I bet Todhunter was served gazpacho soup the second he was on solids. No – he was probably breast-fed with it, from his hoity-toity mum's titty, the other one freely dispensing chilled champagne.

CAT: Is this gonna go on all day? I thought he was going to get wiped.

RIMMER: Yes, turn me off. Get it over with.

LISTER: I've already done it. I wiped the other one.

RIMMER: What? When?

LISTER: Just before you walked in.

RIMMER: And you let me stand here and bare my soul . . .

LISTER: I wanted to find out about the gazpacho soup business, and I knew you wouldn't tell me.

RIMMER: Of course I wouldn't tell you. Because you'd make my life hell with gazpacho soup jokes for the rest of eternity.

LISTER: Rimmer, I swear I will never mention this conversation again. And when I swear, I mean it.

RIMMER: All right. You're a slob, but you keep your word. I believe you. Let's go for a drink.

LISTER: Souper.

Freeze and:

Run credits

CREDITS

GUNMEN OF THE APOCALYPSE

RIMMER   Chris Barrie
LISTER   Craig Charles
CAT   Danny John Jules
KRYTEN   Robert Llewellyn
LORETTA   Jennifer Calvert
SIMULANT CAPTAIN/DEATH   Denis Lil
SIMULANT FEMALE   Liz Hickling
JIMMY   Steve Devereaux

Stunt Co-ordinator   Gerald Naprous
Music   Howard Goodall
Visual FX   Peter Wragg
Video FX   Karl Mooney
Editor   Graham Hutchings
Production Manager   Kerry Waddell
Costume Designer   Howard Burden

Make-up Designer   Andria Pennell
Lighting Director   John Pomphrey
Set Designer   Mel Bibby
Executive Producers   Rob Grant, Doug Naylor
Producer   Justin Judd
Director   Andy De Emmony

HOLOSHIP

RIMMER   Chris Barrie
LISTER   Craig Charles
CAT   Danny John Jules
HOLLY   Hattie Hayridge
KRYTEN   Robert Llewellyn
NIRVANA CRANE   Jane Horrocks
CAPTAIN PLATINI   Matthew Marsh
COMMANDER BINKS   Don Warrington
HARRISON   Lucy Briers

Music   Howard Goodall
Visual FX   Peter Wragg
Editor   Graham Hutchings
Associate Producer   Julian Scott
Costume Designer   Howard Burden
Make-up Designer   Andria Pennell

Lighting Director   John Pomphrey
Set Designer   Mel Bibby
Executive Producers   Rob Grant,
   Doug Naylor
Producer   Hilary Bevan Jones
Director   Juliet May

CAMILLE

RIMMER   Chris Barrie
LISTER   Craig Charles
CAT   Danny John Jules
HOLLY   Hattie Hayridge
KRYTEN   Robert Llewellyn
MECHANOID CAMILLE   Judy Pascoe
HOLOGRAM CAMILLE   Francesca Folan
KOCHANSKI CAMILLE   Suzanne Rhatican

Music   Howard Goodall
Visual FX   Peter Wragg
Editor   Graham Hutchings
Production Manager   Julian Scott
Costume Designer   Howard Burden
Make-up Designer   Andria Pennell

Lighting Director   John Pomphrey
Set Designer   Mel Bibby
Executive Producer   Paul Jackson
Producers   Ed Bye, Rob Grant,
   Doug Naylor
Director   Ed Bye

BACKWARDS

RIMMER	Chris Barrie
LISTER	Craig Charles
CAT	Danny John Jules
HOLLY	Hattie Hayridge
KRYTEN	Robert Llewellyn
WAITRESS	Maria Friedman
MC	Tony Hawks
CUSTOMER	Anna Palmer
MANAGER	Arthur Smith

Stunt Co-ordinator Gareth Milne
Music Howard Goodall
Visual FX Peter Wragg
Editor Ed Wooden
Production Manager Mike Agnew
Costume Designer Howard Burden
Make-up Designer Bethan Jones

Lighting Director John Pomphrey
Set Designer Mel Bibby
Executive Producer Paul Jackson
Producers Ed Bye, Rob Grant, Doug Naylor
Director Ed Bye

KRYTEN

RIMMER   Chris Barrie
LISTER   Craig Charles
CAT   Danny John Jules
HOLLY   Norman Lovett
KRYTEN   David Ross

Music   Howard Goodall
Visual FX   Peter Wragg
Editor   Ed Wooden
Production Manager   Mike Agnew
Costume Designer   Jackie Pinks

Make-up Designer   Bethan Jones
Lighting Director   John Pomphrey
Set Designer   Paul Montague
Executive Producer   Paul Jackson
Producer/Director   Ed Bye

ME²